The Templar Detective and the Code Breaker

A Templar Detective Thriller

Also by J. Robert Kennedy

James Acton Thrillers

The Protocol
Brass Monkey
Broken Dove
The Templar's Relic
Flags of Sin
The Arab Fall
The Circle of Eight
The Venice Code
Pompeii's Ghosts
Amazon Burning
The Riddle
Blood Relics
Sins of the Titanic
Saint Peter's Soldiers
The Thirteenth Legion
Raging Sun
Wages of Sin
Wrath of the Gods
The Templar's Revenge
The Nazi's Engineer
Atlantis Lost
The Cylon Curse
The Viking Deception
Keepers of the Lost Ark
The Tomb of Genghis Khan
The Manila Deception
The Fourth Bible
Embassy of the Empire
Armageddon
No Good Deed

Special Agent Dylan Kane Thrillers

Rogue Operator
Containment Failure
Cold Warriors
Death to America
Black Widow
The Agenda
Retribution
State Sanctioned
Extraordinary Rendition
Red Eagle
The Messenger

Templar Detective Thrillers

The Templar Detective
The Parisian Adulteress
The Sergeant's Secret
The Code Breaker
The Black Scourge
The Unholy Exorcist
The Lost Children

Kriminalinspektor Wolfgang Vogel Mysteries

The Colonel's Wife
Sins of the Child

Delta Force Unleashed Thrillers

Payback
Kill Chain
Infidels
Forgotten
The Lazarus Moment
The Cuban Incident

Detective Shakespeare Mysteries

Depraved Difference
Tick Tock
The Redeemer

Zander Varga, Vampire Detective

The Turned

THE TEMPLAR DETECTIVE AND THE CODE BREAKER

J. ROBERT KENNEDY

UnderMill Press

This is a work of fiction. Names, characters, places, and incidents are products of the author's imagination. Any resemblance to actual persons, living or dead, is entirely coincidental.

ISBN: 9781990418105

First Edition

For our lady,
Notre-Dame de Paris.

The Templar Detective and the Code Breaker

A Templar Detective Thriller

"Thou shalt not lend upon usury to thy brother; usury of money, usury of victuals, usury of any thing that is lent upon usury."

Deuteronomy 23:19, King James Version

"Neither a borrower nor a lender be,
For loan oft loses both itself and friend,
And borrowing dulls the edge of husbandry."

Hamlet Act 1, scene 3, 75–77
William Shakespeare

AUTHOR'S NOTE

This is the fifth novel in this series, and for those who have read the others and embraced these characters as so many of you have, please feel free to skip this note, as you will have already read it.

The word "detective" is believed to have originated in the mid-nineteenth century, however, that doesn't mean the concept of someone who investigated crime originated less than two hundred years ago. Crime long pre-dated this era, and those who investigated it as well.

The following historical thriller is intended to be an entertaining read for all, with the concept of a "Templar Detective" a fun play on a modern term. The dialog is intentionally written in such a way that today's audiences can relate, as opposed to how people might have spoken in Medieval France, where, of course, they would have conversed in French and not English, with therefore completely different manners of speaking, and of addressing one another. For consistency, English phrasing is always used, such as Mister instead of Monsieur, for example. This does not mean they will be speaking to each other as rappers and gangsters, but will instead communicate in ways that imply comfort and familiarity, as we would today. If you are expecting, "Thou dost hath offended me, my good sir," then prepareth thyself for disappointment. If, however, you are looking for a fast-paced adventure, with plenty of action, mystery, and humor, then you've come to the right place.

Enjoy.

PREFACE

At the height of their power, the Templars were estimated to have as many as 2000 mounted knights, and as many as 20,000 additional personnel within the Order. In addition to that, they had over 1000 commanderies, fortresses, outposts, and other properties, among their extensive list of assets.

They were wealthy, almost beyond compare.

Yet sworn to poverty.

Much of this wealth was accumulated over time by the nobles that donated to join or support the cause, but much was also from their ingenious, and perhaps world's first, banking system.

With their sworn mission to protect the pilgrims to the Holy Land from the Saracens and bandits, they soon realized that part of the reason the travelers were targeted was because of the vast amount of wealth they carried with them.

After all, a pilgrimage was a long journey, followed by a usually lengthy stay, before an equally long return home, requiring a large amount of funds to be carried to finance such an endeavor.

Making them ripe pickings for thieves.

Enter the Letter of Credit.

The Templars created a unique system where one could enter a Templar outpost anywhere, deposit a set of assets, then be given a Letter of Credit itemizing those assets, and their value. This letter was encrypted using their unbroken code and given to the traveler, who could then redeem all or part of it along the way to fund their trip.

And it was of little value if stolen.

This ingenious system helped protect the assets of those on a pilgrimage, or traveling anywhere within Europe or the Holy Lands, and reduced the risk to them being raided, as these letters became more commonplace.

The fees charged, and the assets held, including land, made the Templars incredibly wealthy.

And the other religious orders extremely jealous, leaving them desperate to crack the code that protected the world's first international banking system.

Which begs the question: what would have happened if someone had succeeded?

St. Cloud, Kingdom of France
AD 1298

René Courvat stood in front of a solid though simple desk that occupied the center of the entry of the Templar outpost. Sweat trickled down his back and beaded on his upper lip as he futilely attempted slow, steady breaths, his heart still racing despite his desperate efforts. He forced himself to look away from the document now held in the hands of the Templar Knight on duty. The sight of the man's crisp white tunic with large red Maltese cross emblazoned on it, even when viewed only in the periphery of his current tunnel vision, was enough to keep his entire body trembling.

Get a hold of yourself!

He stared at the far corner, nothing but a plain chair occupying it, none of the regalia of the Poor Fellow-Soldiers of Christ and of the Temple of Solomon in sight, his heart finally calming, if only slightly.

"One moment, please," said the knight, an older man whose facial scars suggested a much more exciting youth than the position he now held. As soon as the man was out of sight, René sighed then stopped midway, the sound so loud it had to have been heard in the next room.

Something was wrong.

He had done this before. Many times before. And it had never taken this long.

Something was definitely wrong.

His fingernails dug into his palms, the pain going

unnoticed as he debated leaving.

You should leave. Now!

He started to turn when the door to the back office opened and the elderly knight's head poked through. "I'm terribly sorry. This will only take a few moments." He pointed at the chair in the corner. "Have a seat. It won't be long."

The door closed and René stood, frozen in place.

Would he be so friendly if he knew what you were doing?

He didn't think so.

An innocent man would sit.

He willed his legs to move, and he soon found himself in the chair, with a view of the entire entry of the small Templar outpost less than a day's ride from Paris. The Templars had outposts like this scattered around the massive city, allowing travelers to redeem their Letters of Credit before entering the capital, rather than at the busy Templar fortress.

A place he never intended to go.

The lineups were long, and the chance of greater scrutiny was too much.

And his poor heart could never take the stress.

Yet here, west of the city he lived in, he felt no less insecure.

Though what had he expected? He had pushed his luck. Foolishly. At first, it had simply been the challenge. To think he could do something no one else had been able to do for over a century. It had all started by chance. He had always been good with words and numbers, with figuring out puzzles and recognizing patterns. It was a gift from God, his late mother had told him, and he believed her.

Who else among his friends saw numbers as colors, patterns as smells? Nobody. He was a freak of nature, and kept the source of his unique abilities to himself lest he be declared a demon and find himself tied to a stake.

Though perhaps he was. He *was* different, and it had made his life difficult. He hadn't married, nor would any woman have him. He was simply too awkward. All he had in his life were his younger sisters. They had lost their father several years ago, and their mother soon after. The three were all each other had, and he would do anything to protect them.

And that was why, when he had finally done what none had done before, he had taken advantage of his accomplishment.

His painstakingly achieved accomplishment.

He knew how to read and write, as well as do numbers. It was a skill in short supply where he lived, an area of the city where too many were desperate, and this desperation created a need for his services, services that he charged for, though more often than not took something in trade.

He would read and explain contracts his customers brought to him, usually from loan sharks, though sometimes they would be land contracts, rental agreements, or other forms of agreement made in writing by people of means to people with little. The terms read often brought tears to the eyes of those who had already agreed, their mark at the bottom of the page as meaningless to them as the words above it.

It was heartbreaking work.

But on a number of occasions, he had received old Templar Letters of Credit in exchange for his services, three from the same widow, her husband having traveled to the Holy Land years before, using the Templar network to move his money. In the end, he had died, leaving her nothing but the letters, letters which she had no idea of what they were until she brought them to him to read.

And they were, of course, gibberish, the strange symbols consisting of dots and various lines at different angles, instead of letters and numbers, a code unbroken for so long, it was legend.

But his beautiful mind had noticed patterns, patterns jumping off the pages like deer in the meadows. It had been so obvious, he had immediately realized that each symbol stood for a letter or number, and their use was consistent.

For he was certain the widow's husband's name was repeated near the beginning of each Letter of Credit.

When he informed her they were unreadable, she told him to keep them and feed his fire if he so wished, then left, cursing her dead husband for leaving her with nothing but the clothes on her back.

And it had tortured him that night.

He woke, determined to crack the code and help the widow regain that which her husband hadn't lost, but rather had wisely entrusted to the Templars with their vast network of outposts across Europe and the Holy Land.

The idea was simple. Traveling with sufficient monies to make long journeys, especially to the Holy Land, was foolish. Thieves along the way would prey upon the pilgrims and steal their money. Enter the Templars. At first, they had acted merely as escorts, protecting the pilgrims from thieves and Saracens. But eventually, they developed the concept of Letters of Credit. One's wealth was deposited at a Templar outpost at the beginning of a journey, a Letter of Credit was given indicating the value, then the pilgrim traveled with the piece of paper only. Unless a thief wanted to risk entering an outpost to cash a stolen letter, they were considered not worth the trouble.

When the pilgrim required funds along the way, or finally reached their destination, they could go to any Templar outpost and redeem it, getting as much of the deposited wealth as they required at the time, or all of it should they so desire.

It protected the traveler, and it made the Templars incredibly wealthy by charging fees, or by not having to redeem the Letters of Credit of those who died, their papers lost to the battlefield or the side of the road where they succumbed to brigands or the elements.

And that wealth made many insanely jealous, including monarchs, nobility, and other religious orders.

Yet the Templars, supported by the Pope in Rome, continued to amass tremendous wealth at the expense of the innocent.

And that was why, when he had figured out the code, he hadn't felt any guilt in stealing from them.

Though it had been a challenge. Once he had recognized the pattern and guessed at the letters making up the widow's husband's name, he had to confirm it. He redeemed the Letters, one at a time, then noticed another pattern, indicating what had been deposited, and its value. This had given him even more to work with. He then created his first fake, copying the first letter exactly, but only changing what he was now certain was the name, using only letters he was certain of.

It had worked.

He then took the proceeds, and deposited them at several outposts, having Letters of Credit created for several people, all with a combination of letters that gave him the entire alphabet.

And his brilliant mind had picked out the patterns, and soon had the entire code broken, including every single letter and number. This allowed him to read any Letter of Credit with ease, and he finally took the plunge, creating his own complete forgery, then redeeming it.

It had worked perfectly, and he had given all the funds gained during his experimentation to the widow—anonymously—his guilty conscience settled.

But the victory had been intoxicating, and he had wanted more. Not much, just enough to get by, to make his life, and that of his orphaned sisters, a little better.

Yet today, he was certain he had pushed his luck.

The door opened and he leaped to his feet, the old man returning to his desk, a collection of coins in his hand. He began counting them out, then pushed them toward the still trembling René.

"Sorry for the delay, young man, but we've been short-staffed and I'm getting a little too old for this." He leaned back. "So, how was it?"

René's heart raced. "Sir?"

"The Holy Land."

A trickle of urine raced down his leg as he wondered why the question had been asked.

Because that's the origin you used in the Letter of Credit, you imbecile!

"Oh, umm, it was hot, but inspirational."

The old man chuckled, his head bobbing. "Hot. Oh, I do miss the heat. It's been a long time since I've been there. Things have changed much since I left, I hear."

"I suppose they have." He picked up the coins, his fingers not cooperating with all the shaking, but finally had them all clasped in his hand.

"Are you well? You seem nervous."

René paled. "I-I get this way if I haven't eaten." A coin escaped, dropping to the floor and rolling to his left. He chased it and snagged it before it fell between the floorboards, then held it up, smiling awkwardly. "You, umm, had all my money."

The knight laughed. "Try only being able to carry four *deniers*." He shrugged. "I guess it doesn't matter. The Order takes care of all my needs." He nodded toward the door. "Have a good day."

René bowed with a jerk of his upper body then rushed out the door and into the chilly afternoon, winter still commanding the land. He rushed toward his borrowed horse, stealthily transferring the money gripped in his hand to an inner pocket, hoping no one noticed.

"René! What are you doing here?"

René almost fainted as he recognized the booming voice behind him. It was Enzo, a behemoth of a man that worked for Simone Thibault, a terrifying woman to whom most people he knew owed money. She was a loan shark unlike any other—she was a woman. Her business had been started by her late husband, but upon his death, she had taken over and flourished, the woman as cutthroat as any man.

Especially with beasts like Enzo to do her bidding.

And if this man discovered his secret, not only would he take all the money he had just acquired, he might take his life for not having shared his discovery.

Thibault Residence
Paris, Kingdom of France

Thomas Durant leaned back, his hands clasped across his chest, his eyes closed with a smile as he pictured Isabelle's beautiful face. He hadn't seen her in what felt like months, yet it hadn't been that long.

Though it had been too long to not see the woman he loved.

For he did love her, of that there was no doubt. Isabelle Leblanc was the most beautiful girl he had ever seen, the first he had ever loved, yet to commit to her meant losing everything he had, everything he had ever been.

His mood fouled with the thought, his smile turning into a frown as his heart raced.

Isabelle lived on a farm outside of the city, in the small town of Crécy-la-Chapelle. She lived with her parents, and though they had spoken of her moving to Paris when they got married, there was no possibility she would be happy here. Life was too fast-paced, too cutthroat. She would never survive. He, on the other hand, had grown up here, and knew nothing different. His parents were both dead, and all he had left of them was the house he had grown up in. It wasn't much, as they had been poor, his father's business as a forger of letters and documents not a thriving one.

Though now, now that he worked for the despicable Simone Thibault, he had more money than he had ever known. She paid him well, perhaps too well, as his skills were desperately required, and he had proven trustworthy. That trustworthiness, however, wasn't out of loyalty, but fear. Enzo, her henchman, was twice his size, if not thrice, and could tear him limb from limb, literally, he was certain.

It kept most in line, the few daring to challenge her never doing so again after Enzo entered the room and closed the door.

And it kept him here.

Or did it?

He had a standing invitation from Sir Marcus de Rancourt, a Templar Knight who had taken an interest in him several months ago, and was now a protector of Isabelle, and once the subject of her affections. Sir Marcus and his men were the best examples of honor he had ever encountered, and to be associated with them he was certain would put him in the Lord's good books despite his recent activities.

Yet they lived on a farm, raising Sir Marcus' niece and nephew, along with an orphan they had taken in, and also acting as protectors to Lady Joanne and her former chambermaid, Beatrice. It was a growing group that would welcome him with open arms, yet farming was something that simply didn't interest him.

And didn't pay.

He was ashamed to admit he was obsessed with money. With wealth. With the power and freedom it brought.

He hadn't been hungry since he began working here, which was not something he could have said before. In fact, most of his life had been living on the razor's edge of satiety and starvation. His father had tried his best, but it had never been enough.

If only he could see me now.

His frown deepened.

He'd be ashamed of what I've become.

Though his father wasn't an innocent man, he had never hurt anyone. At least directly. Though Thomas wasn't exactly privy to all his father was up to, there was little doubt someone ultimately got hurt by the masterful forgeries he created.

Not the least of whom was Thomas' own father, murdered by a man he thought his friend, over a forgery no one could know existed.

His chest ached at the too recent memory.

"What's this? I don't pay you to sleep!"

Thomas bolted upright, opening his eyes to find Simone Thibault staring down at him. "Umm, sorry, ma'am, I wasn't sleeping, I was just, thinking of something."

"Well, think on your own time." She snapped her fingers. "Show me the records for René Courvat."

Thomas opened his desk drawer and flipped through the large stack of outstanding loans, finally finding the paper in question. He handed her the ledger, but she didn't take it. She bounced some coins in her hand before tossing them on his desk. "He gave Enzo this today, said it would clear his loan. Is he right?"

Thomas quickly tallied the coins, already knowing René was correct, for the man had a way with numbers that even Thomas, as skilled as he was, could never hope to match. He updated the ledger and nodded. "Yes, ma'am, his loan is paid in full." His eyebrows rose at the date of the agreement. "After so many years!"

Simone scratched her chin. "Now, where does a man like that get this kind of money?"

Thomas shrugged. "Does it matter? He paid his

debt, including the interest. Isn't that a good thing?"

Simone shook her head, a frown creasing her face. "My poor, naïve little boy. Don't you realize we don't want them paying *off* their debts? We want them paying interest for as long as possible. If everyone paid their debts off early, I'd go broke, which means I'd have to get rid of you."

Thomas didn't think that would necessarily be a bad thing, though kept the thought to himself. "What do you want me to do?"

"There's nothing we can do, but let me know if anyone else is paying off their loans quicker than expected. Something's going on, and I want to know what it is."

"Yes, ma'am."

She spun on her heel and left, leaving Thomas uncertain as to what to do, for he already knew the answer to her question. René wasn't the first to have paid off his loan early, and there were others making unusually high payments. These were all people who shouldn't be able to make payments of this size, yet when he went out with Enzo to collect, the excuse almost universally given was that a relative had died, and they would hopefully be paying off their debts soon.

If he were invested in Simone's business of graft and usury, he might have reported the unusual occurrences to her, but he wasn't, and hadn't. And now he feared what might happen if he had to admit he had known all along something was amiss.

Perhaps I should *leave this all behind and live on the farm.*

De Rancourt Residence
Crécy-la-Chapelle, Kingdom of France

"I can honestly say I have never been more sore in my life."

Templar Knight Sir Marcus de Rancourt regarded his youngest though by no means young squire, Jeremy, lying on his back on the grass, his limbs spread-eagle, every square inch of him covered in dirt and worse.

"It sucks to be the low-man, doesn't it?"

Jeremy's head lifted off the ground and he gave his friend and fellow squire, David, a look. "If there are a thousand rungs on the ladder of seniority, I'm the bottom one, and you're the one above, so don't go acting so superior."

"Hey, if you're on the first rung, and I'm on the second, that means I'm twice as senior as you."

"Yes, but it also means that someone is five-hundred times your senior!"

"I can live with that, as long as I'm twice as senior as you."

"You're an idiot."

"That's Senior Idiot to you."

"You're so stupid, you actually think that's a compliment to yourself."

David shrugged. "Or am I so smart, you simply can't understand my genius?"

Marcus exchanged a glance with his sergeant and trusted friend, Simon Chastain. "Sometimes I miss the separation of knights and squires that we enjoyed in the

Holy Land."

Simon grunted. "If I chopped a few of those rungs off this ladder, I wonder if I might be granted some silence."

Jeremy propped up on his elbows. "Be careful. You're not that far up the ladder yourself." He looked at Marcus. "Don't worry, sir, you're at least on the five-hundredth rung."

"Lovely. So, when the shit rolls downhill, I still get half of it on me."

"Better than all of it like these two." Simon waved a hand in front of his nose. "Speaking of, have you two been shoveling it again?"

David collapsed onto his back, groaning. "It never ends. Day in and day out, those animals shit. That's all they do! They eat and shit and we have to shovel it."

Simon flicked a wrist at the field they had been preparing for spring planting. "And soon you'll be spreading it."

"Ugh, that's going to make this place smell just wonderful."

Marcus chuckled. "Well, the Holy Land didn't smell much better, at least in the cities."

"True, but this is the country. Fresh air, clean water, rolling hills. Yet in a few weeks, it's all going to smell like an outhouse."

Jeremy dropped back onto the grass. "Yes, but in the end it will all be worth it when we harvest our crops."

Simon growled. "That's assuming there's anything to harvest. It's not like we actually know what we're doing."

Marcus smiled. "We'll learn, and there are plenty of people in the village who will answer our questions."

"Only because you're five hundred rungs up Jeremy's ladder."

David rolled over onto his side, propping his head up with his hand. "I think they're actually scared of you."

Marcus eyed him. "If they're scared of anyone, it's Simon." He turned to his friend. "You really need to try smiling more."

Simon frowned. "I tried. It hurt."

They all laughed then fell silent as the door to the farmhouse swung open and Lady Joanne charged out, her former chambermaid, Beatrice, on her heels along with the children and the farm's mastiff, Tanya. Joanne wagged a finger at them. "What are you four doing, lazing about? There's work to be done!"

Jeremy sat up. "Uh, oh. Here comes the thousandth rung."

David snickered and Marcus forced a straight face as Simon cracked a smile, evidently willing to risk the pain.

She came to a sudden halt, grimacing. "Ugh! You know you're supposed to shovel it, not roll around in it?"

Jeremy's mouth fell open and his eyes widened, jabbing a finger at David. "I *told* you we were doing it wrong!"

David rolled to a seated position. "Is that what those big long spoons are for? What did I hear them call it? Sho-vel?"

Lady Joanne glared at them. "You two just might find yourselves without dinner if you keep it up."

The two squires bowed their heads. "Sorry."

"We're heading into the village. I have business there then will be spending some time with Mrs. Leblanc and Isabelle. When I get back, I expect to see you all working."

Marcus rose and bowed slightly. "I can assure you, Milady, we will be hard at it until it is time for dinner."

"Good." She stared at the squires. "And you two better give yourselves a good scrubbing before I see you again." She eyed Marcus and Simon. "And you two as well. I thought Templars were noted for their cleanliness."

Marcus smiled. "We are, Milady, though not while we toil."

"Is that what you call this laziness?" She batted a hand at them. "I'm late. I'll see you at dinner."

She charged off with the children, Beatrice flashing them a grin, Jeremy staring after her ample bosom. David threw a rock at him.

"Could you *be* any more obvious?"

Jeremy shrugged. "I think she likes me."

"What's not to like. She's got a great view from her rung, way above yours."

"Help! Fire! Fire!"

The frivolity ended as Marcus swung toward the distant cry, spotting smoke to the east, farther out of the village. A small boy raced past the farm, shouting his warning. Marcus pointed to the barn. "Get all the buckets you can carry!" The others rushed to execute his order as Marcus hailed the boy. "Boy! Where's the fire?"

"Mr. Pevra's farm. The barn is on fire! A horse

kicked over a lantern!" He continued on, and Marcus sprinted toward the smoke in the distance, joining those already heading to help. *This* was what he loved about this place. Everyone was willing to help in times of need.

They reached the farm to find the fire contained to the barn, though the flames threatened the nearby farmhouse. A bucket brigade had been set up from the river to the barn, water now thrown ineffectually at the blaze, the cries of panicked animals trapped inside stabbing at his heart.

Two men dragged Mr. Pevra from the blaze as he cried out for someone to save the animals. Marcus removed his tunic and grabbed a bucket filled with water. He soaked the shirt then tied it around his head, covering his mouth and nose, the others following suit as he charged toward the barn, kicking open the doors.

A wall of heat greeted him, the flames licking past him as he fell backward and onto the ground. David grabbed him, hauling him to his feet as Simon and Jeremy charged past. Marcus rushed after them, shielding himself with a raised hand, trying to make out the layout through the thick smoke. Animals locked in their pens cried out all around him, and he pushed to the closest stall, hauling it open and stumbling inside, smacking the horse it contained on the ass, sending it charging forward and out of the barn to safety.

He moved to the next stall as he spotted his comrades doing the same around him, animals rushing for freedom and safety as they cleared each stall, others from the village now tossing the water directly through the doors, soaking the straw-covered ground, giving them an escape route that he feared they would need any moment.

He swatted the behind of a squealing pig that refused to move, then gave the massive creature a shove, finally revealing the source of her reluctance.

Six piglets, lying beside her. He grabbed them, piling them in his arms then rushed outside, the sow following, and he handed them off.

Then he spun around at a horrendous sound and gasped as the roof began to collapse.

"Everyone out!" he shouted, the villagers retreating as he strode forward, peering into the smoke and flame as more animals rushed past. "David! Jeremy! Simon! Get out now! The roof—"

His heart leaped into his throat as the entire structure collapsed, starting at the back. A rush of smoke and debris billowed toward him, then he was hit by something large that knocked him off his feet.

It was Jeremy. His squire grinned. "What's it like on the bottom?"

David dropped beside them, face down as Marcus shoved Jeremy off him and struggled back to his feet.

"Simon!"

He rushed toward the flames, but David and Jeremy held him back. Suddenly he heard something, a horse, rushing toward them from the inky blackness. The beast's head emerged from the roiling smoke, directly in front of them. Marcus shoved David and Jeremy out of the way then dropped to his knee as his sergeant, atop the animal, charged over him, the hooves missing by a hair's breadth.

Marcus rose and turned as Simon dismounted. "I thought we had lost you."

"You almost did, but I threatened to cook her over

my fire tonight if she didn't move." He patted the animal on the neck. "That got her going."

Marcus smacked his friend on the back then turned to watch as the villagers gathered up the animals they had saved, Pevra rushing toward them, his hands outstretched.

"Oh, thank you, Sir Marcus, thank you! If it weren't for you and your men, we would have lost everything!"

Sir Marcus shook the man's hand. "Think nothing of it. You would have done the same for us, I'm sure."

The man looked away. "I'm ashamed to say I think I'd be too much the coward."

Marcus patted him on the back. "There's no shame in not rushing into a burning barn. It just shows you're not a fool like us."

Pevra smiled. "You are a good man, Sir Marcus."

"As are you." He turned as the last wall of the barn collapsed, the villagers resuming the bucket brigade. He turned back to Pevra. "We'll come by tomorrow to help you clear away the debris then rebuild." He raised his voice. "If we all work together, and donate a little bit of our time despite the season, we can have Mr. Pevra back on his feet in no time."

Heads bobbed around him, though some seemed reluctant. It was a difficult time. Almost any other time of the year, with the exception of harvest time, would have been better. Spring planting and harvesting were the busiest times on a farm, and he was asking them to give up some of that.

"Now, can anyone donate some barn space for these animals? We'll take the horses, since we have expertise in that area."

"I'll take the pigs!" shouted someone, and within

moments, the rescued animals had new temporary homes.

Satisfied, Marcus led the others back home, all four exhausted, singed, and even filthier than before. Jeremy collapsed on the grass first, followed by David then Simon. Marcus took a knee, then fell to his side. "Well, that was interesting."

"I thought I told you to get to work!"

Marcus rolled over to see Lady Joanne and Beatrice rushing toward them.

"And my God, you're even filthier than before! What the devil have you been up to?"

Marcus opened his mouth to defend his men then decided against it. He was simply too tired.

"Well?"

"I'll explain everything later."

Lady Joanne wagged a finger. "You know, there was a fire at Mr. Pevra's farm. The least you could have done was gone and helped the poor man."

She stormed off to the farmhouse, leaving the four of them to their exhaustion.

Jeremy sighed. "I think the view from the thousandth rung isn't so good."

Courvat Residence
Paris, Kingdom of France

René Courvat stared at the fruits of his labor, another forged Templar Letter of Credit. Though he was now expert in their code, it was his fear that made the work painstaking, for he would review it over and over, never certain he hadn't made some critical error that would have him found out and arrested.

Then hanged.

All for a pittance. This latest forgery would barely feed a nobleman for a day, yet it would mean everything to the person he had created it for, another fool like himself who had borrowed from Simone Thibault in desperation.

But unlike most, he had found a way out, his debt cleared only days ago, much to the annoyance of Simone, he was certain.

And that delighted him to no end.

It was a loan shark like Simone that had killed his father several years ago when he had paid a doctor to look at his youngest sister rather than make his weekly payment on his insurmountable debt. The murder had destroyed his mother, and hadn't left the family off the hook. She died soon after of a broken heart and stress, he was certain.

Leaving him and his two sisters all alone in the world.

His debt had been bought out by Simone for some reason, and he had struggled to make every payment since, for the sake of his young sisters. Should he be killed, God only knew what would happen to them.

And now his family was finally free of the debt, and the only ones hurt were the fabulously rich Templars, with so much money he was certain they would never notice, or if they did, care. The Templars were powerful. Rich. And they profited handsomely off the backs of those who would travel to and from the Holy Land. Personally, he found it immoral to charge these exorbitant fees simply so people could travel without fear of losing all their possessions to bandits.

The Templars had been founded to protect pilgrims from marauding Muslims who were constantly robbing and killing Christians on a spiritual journey, and they had done a fine job of it. And expanding their protection to lower the risk of valuables being stolen along the way by issuing Letters of Credit was ingenious, and he never would have begrudged them a small administrative fee.

But that wasn't what was happening. If it were, then the Templars wouldn't be so rich. They wouldn't be one of the largest landowners in the world, they wouldn't have the finest horses and equipment. They wouldn't be monks, sworn to poverty, living far better lives than he and his neighbors. It enraged him every time he saw one of the knights, in their crisp white surcoats with bright red cross emblazoned across their chests, riding a fully equipped horse, their heads held high with pride as the crowds parted in awe to let them and their entourages through. Their good lives were built on the backs of those very souls who showed them such reverence, and it sickened him.

That was why, when he had noticed the pattern,

when he had discovered a way to perhaps take back some of that which the Templars had taken, and do some good with it, he had jumped at the opportunity.

Even if it meant certain death in the end should he be caught.

The first time he had stolen from the holy order, it had been terrifying, and for a pittance of an amount. Should he have been found out, he had hoped the insignificant sum would have merited a slap on the wrist and a stern word rather than arrest. And when it had worked, he traveled around the small towns outside Paris, redeeming his forged Letters of Credit, made out to different names in small amounts so as to not attract attention, and within a matter of months, had paid back Simone, the final payment only just extracted from him by the beast that worked for her.

I much prefer Thomas.

The young man was clearly a reluctant pawn, and he had a feeling might be wise to the fact something was going on. And if he was, he might feel obligated to tell his mistress. That could prove dangerous, for should she find out what he was doing, he had no doubt she would force him to work for her, defrauding the Templars of a portion of their tremendous wealth something irresistible to a woman like her.

And then they would be found out, for soon even his little operation would be discovered. For the books wouldn't balance. The distances slowed things down, as all his forgeries claimed he was returning from the Holy Land, or some distant outpost like Rome, so it could take months, perhaps a year before the first fraud might be caught. And even if it were, records would then be double-checked and messages exchanged, all over great distances, such that he figured he had a minimum of a year in which he could successfully get away with things, perhaps even two.

But only if he didn't become greedy and attract attention.

There was a knock on his door. "Come in."

His youngest sister, Grace, entered. "Mrs. Fromont is here to see you."

He sighed, closing his eyes. Fromont had been the first he had helped, and not the last. He couldn't help himself, and in time, it would lead to his downfall. He was a fool for a pretty lady, especially one that reminded him of his sisters and what they would soon face as they were forced out into the cruel world that was the Kingdom of France. "Show her in."

How much would it be this time? And would this be the one that had them all brought up on charges before the King? He had to put an end to it, but he had no idea how, for Pandora's Box had been opened, and it could never be closed again.

The Shrieking Owl Tavern
Paris, Kingdom of France

Hamon Pequin watched as Girard Fromont counted out the coins, placing each atop the previous, creating a small stack in front of him. It was a pittance of a sum to Pequin, but an impossible amount for someone such as Fromont to possess.

Something was wrong.

He charged exorbitant interest on his loans for a reason. He never wanted them paid off. It kept him living far better than those around him, and financed his operation, an operation that didn't come cheap. With a dozen men working for him, collecting on his debts, he had officially made it. He could sit here, in a tavern he owned, all day and all night, enjoying the company of those loyal to him, and women he essentially owned who would fulfill any desire he might have.

It was the life he had always dreamed of, and it was a life he'd do anything to protect.

There was no way he would go back to the way things had been. He had grown up poor, dirt poor, like everyone else in this godforsaken neighborhood. But he had an advantage over the others. He had a father who had no scruples, no morals, no boundaries. He would lie, steal, cheat—whatever it took to keep his family fed.

Then, shortly before his untimely death, he had discovered the genius of loan sharking. He began pouring his ill-gotten gains into high-interest loans to desperate neighbors, and it had changed everything, if only for a couple of years before one of those desperate souls killed him rather than pay.

It had been a valuable lesson.

Pequin took over the business, but surrounded himself with local goons, sending them to do the dirty work, protecting him from the crazed determined to escape their debts. His men were rarely hurt, for killing the collector meant nothing, and his debtors knew it.

And his business, built on the backs of the starving and struggling, grew substantially over the years to the empire it was today.

With him sitting atop the pile of wealth he had accumulated, most of it loaned out to the neighborhood, their weekly payments providing him a lifestyle as close to nobility as one could expect in the rat-infested shacks of these slums.

It was a good life.

A life that depended on people like Fromont *not* paying off their debts.

"Tell me, where did you get the money?"

Fromont placed the last coin on the table, then stood straight. "My brother. He died and left me a small legacy."

Pequin gestured toward the impressive stack of coins. "Not so small, to pay off a loan so soon."

Fromont shifted from one foot to the other. "He had a, umm, better life than me. He was a, umm, blacksmith."

Pequin regarded him for a moment. "I don't believe you."

Fromont's eyes bulged as he paled. "I-I'm telling the truth! I swear!"

Pequin folded his arms. "No, you're not." He narrowed his eyes, boring into those of his former debtor. "Where'd you get the money? Did you steal it? I don't want someone coming to me tomorrow saying I have what's his because you're a thief."

Fromont shook his head vehemently. "No, I swear, I didn't steal it!"

"If your brother left you a legacy, then there must be some proof. A letter, something." He reached forward and knocked over the stack of coins with a flick of a finger. "These are fine silver." He pursed his lips, folding his arms once again. "I think you robbed a man of his purse. Perhaps a nobleman." He glared at Fromont, his voice lowering to a growl. "I want the truth now, or I'll have my men beat it out of you."

Fromont went ghost-white. "No, I can't, I promised. Please don't make me! It will ruin everything!"

One side of Pequin's mouth curled into a sneer. "Now I'm *very* intrigued." He signaled his men to move in. "Let's find out what it is you're so willing to die to protect."

Courvat Residence
Paris, Kingdom of France

René yawned, his eyelids heavy, the candlelight no longer sufficient to allow him to continue his work. He stretched, all four limbs extended as far as they could go, then sighed as his entire body relaxed.

Grace giggled.

He turned in his chair, giving her a judging eye. "Do I make you laugh?"

"Yes."

"Is it because I look funny?"

"Yes."

"Is it because I look silly?"

"Yes!"

"Well, which is it, then? It can't be both!"

"Yes, it can!"

He pursed his lips, giving her a quizzical look. "So, you're saying I look funny *and* silly."

"I am!"

"Huh. Well, you're my sister, and I know my sister would never lie, so then it must be true." He faked a pout. "I don't want to look funny *and* silly." His chin sagged. "One is fine, but not both."

Grace rushed from her perch at the window and leaped into his lap. "Pick one!"

He scrunched up his nose. "I think I'd rather look silly than funny."

She grabbed both his cheeks then leaned back, assessing his face. "I take it back. You just look silly."

He smiled. "Good! Silly I can live with!" He gave her a big hug then put her back on the floor. "Now, how about we go see what our sister has cooked us for dinner."

"It smells delicious!" His sister rushed for the door. "We always eat like kings when you return from your trips."

He smiled, staring at the latest forgery on his desk. Being forced to pay off Simone early had dealt their finances a serious blow, though in the end it would be worth it. But it also meant leaving sooner than planned to collect some more of his ill-gotten gains.

Someone hammered on the door downstairs and his eldest sister, Vivienne, screamed. He pointed to the bed in the corner. "Get under there, now! Don't make a sound!"

Grace's trembling body shook out a nod, the terror in her eyes heartbreaking, her legs doing nothing to fulfill his demands. He pushed her toward the bed and she scrambled under it, receding into the darkest corner of the room. He reached for his door, heavy footfalls on the stairs, and gasped as it flew open, a man far more terrifying than Simone entering.

"René! I don't believe we've formally met. Do you know who I am?"

He nodded. "Mr. Pequin."

"Good! I always like it when my reputation precedes me." Hamon Pequin leaned slightly closer as two of his henchmen entered, Alain and Lyon, both men René's age he recognized from the neighborhood, having grown up with both. "It means I have to explain myself much less."

He resisted the urge to look at the bed as Alain sat

on it then stretched out, Lyon taking a perch on Grace's favorite windowsill. "How-how can I help you?"

Pequin motioned toward René's chair. "May I?" He sat before René could reply, sighing as he leaned back and stared up at him. "You've been holding out on me, my boy."

His heart hammered as he knew immediately what this was about, his worst fears about to come true. "Wh-what do you mean?"

"Mr. Fromont told me everything. About how you've cracked the Templar code and have been creating fake Letters of Credit."

He decided saying nothing was best.

"Do you deny it?"

"I-I—"

Pequin tapped his finger on the latest forgery, still sitting on the desk.

His shoulders slumped. "No."

"Excellent." Pequin rose. "You're working for me now."

His eyes bulged. "I-I can't! We'll get caught! I have my sisters to think of!"

Pequin came within a few inches of René's face. "Exactly." He jabbed a finger into René's chest. "Cross me, and they're dead. Understood?"

Tears filled his eyes as he realized it was all over. The wrong person had found out, and now things were out of his control. His chin sagged to his chest. "Yes."

"Excellent." Pequin headed for the door, beckoning Alain and Lyon to follow. "Oh, and René?"

He turned. "Yes?"

"You can tell your sister to come out from under

the bed now. I have no intention of hurting either one of them." He glared at him. "So long as you do everything I say."

He stood trembling as they left, their footfalls fading away with the slamming of the front door. Vivienne bolted up the stairs as Grace rolled out from under the bed, both rushing into his arms, wailing, and it was everything he could do to maintain control over his own fears.

Instead, he held them tight, whispering assurances to them that even he didn't believe.

For all was now lost.

Pequin pulled his collar higher against the cold, staring back at René's humble home, one that reminded him of what he had grown up in. He knew the man from the neighborhood, though calling him a man was an insult to them all. René was awkward, weak, and would never know the pleasures of a woman unless he paid for it.

Perhaps if he does well, I'll send over one of the girls.

He chuckled at the notion.

"What's so-so funny, boss?" asked Alain, a true idiot if there ever was one. The only reason he kept the stuttering fool around was that he was unquestionably loyal, incredibly strong, and extremely fast. He was the perfect tool.

"Just thinking if things work out, René might finally get a woman."

Lyon grinned. "I don't think he'd know what to do with one. He'd probably spend his time counting all her parts!"

Alain roared with laughter, Pequin joining in as he

imagined the awkward man doing just that. He raised a finger, ending the laughter. He pointed back at the house. "That man is the key to our future, gentlemen. Nobody must know what's going on, and nothing can ever happen to him." He stopped, turning toward them. "It's your job to protect him."

Lyon nodded. "Umm, what if the Templars find out?"

Pequin resumed walking. "I don't care. Everything will point to him. But if a Templar gets too close, kill him."

Alain's eyes shot wide. "K-kill a Templar?"

Pequin glanced at him, the fear on his face the most intelligent expression the boy had ever made. "If you don't think you can handle it, then leave now."

Alain shook his head, his eyes bulging at the very notion. "I-I can handle it."

"Good. Because nobody ever leaves once they start working for me." He paused, giving Alain the eye. "At least not breathing."

De Rancourt Residence
Crécy-la-Chapelle, Kingdom of France
Three months later

"While I live and breathe, I never thought the stories I heard could ever be true!"

Sir Marcus de Rancourt turned toward the voice, a voice he recognized all too well. And a smile broke out. "Damase! I can't believe it!" He tossed his spade aside and rushed down the hill toward one of his oldest friends, Sir Damase de Sissey. "What are you doing here?"

"Looking to see with my own eyes that which my ears didn't believe. That the greatest warrior the Order has ever known is now working a farm."

Marcus embraced the man, giving him a thumping hug before stepping back and apologizing. "Forgive me for my condition. Working a farm is dirty work."

"Smelly as well." Sir Damase smiled as Marcus' crusty old sergeant approached. "So, you old fool, you decided to stay with him?"

"I did." Simon shook the man's hand as David and Jeremy rushed over, excitement on their faces at the sight of an old friend from their days in the Order. "What brings you here?"

"Today? Curiosity. Tomorrow, after I depart, business."

"Where do they have you stationed now?"

"I'm in Rome. Accounts."

Marcus frowned, eying the man's shoulder. "So,

your wound never recovered?"

Damase shook his head. "No, and with it being the right shoulder, I just can't swing a sword like I used to." He gestured toward Marcus'. "And your wound?"

"I wouldn't say fully recovered, but it's held its own since I've arrived."

Damase chuckled. "I can't see that you'd have much opportunity to test it in these parts."

Marcus rolled his eyes. "You'd be surprised at what we've managed to get mixed up in."

Simon jerked a thumb at his master. "You know him. He's always sticking his nose into something he shouldn't be."

"I *do* know him, and I can only imagine." Damase gestured toward the barracks at the top of the hill. "I assume that's where you are living rather than in this comfortable farmhouse?" He gestured toward the house at the bottom of the hill, the sound of women and children rolling over the fields.

"It is. There's no room in the house for any of us now."

Damase frowned. "I heard of your sister. You have my condolences."

"Thank you, old friend." Marcus gestured to Jeremy who quickly took charge of Damase's horse, leading it toward the barn with David. "You're staying with us tonight, I hope?"

"If I'm welcome."

Marcus chuckled. "You are always welcome here, my friend, after everything we've been through together." They entered the barracks, the warmth of the fire welcome, the three of them sitting in front of the stone hearth, its radiated heat soothing his aching bones.

David entered, carrying Damase's possessions, placing them on one of the beds. "Your belongings, sir. Can I help you out of your armor?"

Damase nodded, standing and stretching out his arms, David expertly removing the chainmail and outer garments, leaving the friends only moments later to talk in private. "You have good boys there."

Simon grunted. "Hardly boys anymore. They certainly stink like men."

Damase squinted. "I'm afraid you all do. Do you not bathe in France?"

"Not as much as in the Order, unfortunately, though this is more a function of the work we've been doing." Marcus regarded his friend. "So, what brings you here? You said you were in accounts?"

"Something curious. I've noticed some irregularities in our bookkeeping for the past several months. I've been sent to consult with the fortress in Paris since the transactions all seem to tie back here."

"What kind of irregularities?"

Damase glanced about, as if making sure they were alone, the only other "person" in the room Tanya, the farm's mastiff. "I believe our code has been broken."

"Impossible!" cried Simon. "That can't be!"

Marcus had to agree. "Are you certain?"

Damase sighed. "No, but I can't think of any other explanation."

"What is your evidence?"

"What appear to be forged Letters of Credit."

Marcus leaned forward. "Explain."

"We've been receiving copies of redeemed Letters

of Credit that indicate they were issued in Rome. As you know, once a Letter has been redeemed and paid out, the original is sent to the regional headquarters, and a copy is made and returned to the originating outpost, so that it can be balanced against our books."

"And these forgeries? They don't match?"

Damase shook his head. "No, they don't. There are no records of any of them having come from our end."

Simon pursed his lips, folding his arms, clearly not convinced. "Perhaps someone screwed up."

"Once, maybe. Twice? Perhaps. But over a dozen times? No, definitely not."

Marcus felt slightly sickened. "Is the breaking of our code the only way this could have been done?"

"It is the only way I dare consider, for the only other is that one of our own is behind it."

Simon chewed his cheek. "That sounds more reasonable than our code having been broken."

Damase sighed. "Yes, it does, but to what end? The amounts are trivial in nature, at least until recently. And every single one of the redemptions has taken place around Paris. That would mean he would have to be stationed here, and run the risk of being recognized." He shook his head. "No, I don't think one of our own is behind this."

Marcus frowned. "I hope you're wrong. Otherwise, it does mean the code has been broken."

Simon shrugged. "Does it really matter, though? Just change the code."

Damase's eyes widened slightly. "You don't understand, do you?"

Simon grunted. "Evidently not."

"Let me explain. If the code has been broken, it could undermine the entire system. If our Letters of Credit can't be trusted, it all collapses."

Simon appeared skeptical. "How?"

"If word of this gets out, it could mean the end of the Order itself."

Simon exchanged a glance with Marcus. "Again, how?"

"The bulk of our income outside of donations comes from our Letters of Credit system. The fees we charge, and the rents we charge on assets held as collateral, are what fund the entire Order. It is a massive undertaking, and exceptionally expensive. If those that use our system lose confidence in it, it could collapse very quickly, and we'd lose all that income. We would be unable to maintain our current holdings, be forced to liquidate assets to pay our bills, and eventually, to shrink our numbers dramatically. In the end, we would be left with nothing. The Order would be no more."

Marcus frowned. "While I don't share your doom and gloom assessment, I do agree the situation is severe. You are absolutely right that if confidence were lost, and the system was to fail, we would be reduced considerably. I would hope that the nobles of Europe would continue to fund us through donations as they join our ranks, though you're right, the extent of our influence would be dramatically reduced."

Damase sighed. "I'm afraid you're forgetting one thing."

"What's that?"

"If we are so greatly reduced and disgraced, we risk being taken over by another order."

Simon growled. "You don't mean the Hospitallers,

do you?"

"Exactly. You know how they are. If they sensed weakness, and dishonor, they would petition Rome for our disbandment, and eventual absorption."

Marcus' chest tightened at the thought. "That can't be allowed to happen." He leaned closer to his friend. "Does anyone know about this?"

"Very few. The amounts were trivial until recently, though are still not enough to raise concern beyond the possible implications of how it is being done."

"This recent change, do you think he's become greedier?"

"Possibly. And if he continues, the amounts could become too big to hide."

Marcus frowned. "How can we help?"

"Provide me with a hot meal, some good company, and a roof over my head until morning."

"You have it."

Damase smiled slightly. "And a prayer to wish me well?"

Marcus laughed, patting his friend on the back. "You shall have that too. And should you need us, all you need to do is ask."

Courvat Residence
Paris, Kingdom of France

"It's too much! They'll figure it out!"

René cringed as Pequin glared at him, clearly displeased with his objections. It had been months now since he had been forced to work for Pequin, the amounts initially small like he had been doing, then progressively larger as time went on, their crimes unnoticed, or at least unsolved.

And every time he expressed his fears, Pequin would point to Grace and Vivienne, both forced to stand in the room each time Pequin would visit with his next demand. They were under constant threat, and he had no idea how to get out from under this, though if he didn't, they would all end up caught and hanged.

Then who will take care of them?

They needed husbands. It would solve everything should something happen to him, and perhaps was where his focus should lie. They were both pretty. Vivienne could cook like no one's business, making any meager meal a feast, and she was teaching the younger Grace. Vivienne at least was nearly of the age where marriage could be considered, though just. Grace had years before he'd let her, though he was certain there were perverts out there who would happily bed her.

He stared at Pequin, ogling his sisters, the man clearly one of the perverts he feared. "You're going to get us all killed."

Pequin turned his attention back to René. "Talk like that will get your sisters killed." He leaned closer. "Or worse."

René's heart raced, his mouth going dry. "You wouldn't dare."

Pequin smiled sinisterly. "I wouldn't, no, but some of my men?" He shrugged. "Who knows what they might do if they knew your sisters were no longer under my protection?"

René struggled to maintain control. "Is that what you call it? Protection?"

"They remain untouched so long as you do what I say. No longer." He jabbed him with a finger. "And the longer it takes for you to fully grasp that, the more impatient I become."

René's shoulders slumped, defeated. "But you ask for too much! These amounts are too high to go unnoticed. Eventually, they'll discover the imbalance, and investigate. Then we're doomed."

Pequin leaned back. "I fail to see how. No real names are used, and the forgeries are always redeemed outside of Paris by different people. I fail to see, even if they figure out what is going on, how they might ever find out who's behind it. We are perfectly safe, as long as you don't panic."

"But they might begin refusing the Letters of Credit if they find out we're forging them."

Pequin chuckled. "Ahh, my young friend, you are so naïve. Don't you realize what's going on here?"

René frowned. "I guess not."

"My boy, there is nothing they can possibly do about it."

"What do you mean?"

"If word ever got out that their system has been

compromised, it would collapse immediately. The Templars would be finished. All Letters of Credit would be suspect, and it would ruin them. They would collapse financially, lose the backing of the royal families of Europe, and most importantly, the Pope and the Roman Catholic Church." Pequin leaned closer. "René, my boy, they can't say or do anything, beyond hope to get lucky." A sly grin emerged. "And luck is always on my side."

Paris, Kingdom of France

Simone Thibault frowned as she regarded Pequin, the uncouth bastard sporting a hat far finer than anything she had previously seen him in. In fact, his entire wardrobe appeared out of place. It was a bit of the pot calling the kettle black arse, however, since she too was dressed far above her true station, though that was to separate her from the masses she leeched off.

And the fact Pequin too was separating himself, suggested his business had taken a turn for the better.

"Mrs. Thibault, a pleasure to see you this fine day."

She forced a smile. "And you, Mr. Pequin. That's a fine hat you're wearing."

He bowed slightly, tipping it. "It is, isn't it? And yours is lovely as well."

She didn't bother to curtsy. "Business must be good to afford such fine attire."

"It is, thank you. As yours obviously continues to be."

She regarded his entourage, never smaller than half a dozen. "Perhaps if you didn't have so many men draining your purse, you'd be able to afford a finer pair of shoes."

Pequin frowned, staring down at his humble shoes, the one piece of his wardrobe the galoot had neglected. His cheeks flushed. "You should watch your tongue while alone on the street. Enzo isn't here to protect you."

She smiled. "I'll tell him you said that. That way he'll

know if anything ever happens to me, *you* are the one to pay a visit to."

Pequin gulped, the prospect of a visit from her primary enforcer evidently unwelcome. He tipped his hat. "Ma'am, it's been pleasant, but I have business to attend to."

She smiled. "As do I." She pointed behind them as Enzo rounded the corner. "Oh, here's Enzo now. Perhaps you'd like to pay your respects?"

Pequin's voice shot up a couple of octaves. "That won't be necessary!" He rushed off, his men stumbling after him as they kept a wary eye on the lumbering mass of approaching muscle.

"Is everything fine, ma'am?"

She nodded as Pequin and his lackeys fled. "Something is going on there. There's no way a man like that can afford clothes such as those. He's on to something. We need to find out what."

"How?"

She thought for a moment, her lips pursed as the last of them disappeared around the corner, likely heading back to the tavern that acted as their headquarters. She smiled. "Grab one of his men tonight when they leave the bar. Get him even drunker. Find out what he knows."

"And if he won't talk?"

"Tenderize him a bit if you have to. Whatever Pequin is up to, I want in." She glanced down at her clothes. "I've been needing a new dress for ages, but all my money is tied up with ungrateful debtors who think I'm the bad one for them getting into trouble." She shook her head, resuming her trek home. "What a world we live in, when a hard working woman like me is considered evil by those she sacrifices for."

"It's terrible. What would these vermin do without you to help them?"

She smiled up at the big man. "I'm so happy I have you, Enzo. I think you're the only one who truly understands the sacrifices I make for my fellow Parisians." She patted him on the back. "Now, go get one of those bastards drunk and find out what's going on." She paused. "And take Thomas with you. Let him ask the questions. Your strengths lie elsewhere."

Enclos du Temple, Templar Fortress
Paris, Kingdom of France

"What have you found?"

Sir Damase de Sissey gestured toward the pile of papers sitting on Sir Matthew Norris' desk. "Our books aren't reconciling. We've been sent notices of Letters of Credit being redeemed in your region, that apparently originated in Rome, that we never issued."

Sir Matthew flipped through the pages. "A bookkeeping error?"

Damase shook his head. "No, that's what we thought at first, but there are too many errors, and they've been getting bigger and more frequent. The only pattern we've been able to discern is that they are all redeemed within a day's ride of Paris, but never inside Paris."

"Interesting."

"And disturbing. I suggest we put a message out to all our outposts to see if anyone else has noticed this pattern. I can't believe whoever is behind this would only target Rome."

Matthew continued scanning the pages. "The amounts, even now, are trivial, though I'll concede they are growing." He regarded Damase. "Are you making too much of this?"

Damase tensed. For the Templar Master for France to not see the significance was stunning, yet pointing that out would have to be done delicately. "Sir, I don't think you, umm, grasp what is going on."

Matthew smiled slightly, leaning back and folding his arms, Damase's word choice evidently poor. "Enlighten me."

Damase drew a deep breath, steeling for the defense of his position, something he had already done with this man's counterpart in Rome. "Sir, someone has broken our code. *Everything* is now at risk. Not only our Letters of Credit, but our entire communications network. Nothing is safe. Before today, we always assumed that if a messenger was intercepted, no one would be able to read our correspondence. But now? Anyone can."

Matthew raised a finger slightly. "Only if it has been shared. I would think if anyone figured out our code, they would keep it to themselves so they could benefit, as they have been. Why share this information and risk getting found out? And besides, we can always change the code."

Damase's heart beat a little quicker as he tensed, his point not getting through. "Sir, that would only stop them temporarily, I fear. If they figured out how to crack the code once, then they can do it again." He tapped the stack of forged Letters of Credit. "Look at these initial transactions we flagged. These names are unusual. They're obviously designed to cover every letter of the alphabet."

Matthew leaned forward, picking up the pages to see for himself. His eyes widened slightly.

"Whoever is behind this is smart. *Very* smart. Simply changing the code isn't going to stop him. But there's a bigger thing at stake here."

Matthew tossed the pages back on his desk. "Bigger than our financial system being pillaged?"

"Yes." Damase lowered his voice slightly. "Sir, if

word gets out that our code has been broken, that our Letters of Credit are suspect, then the entire system could fail. No one will want to entrust us with their assets for fear someone at the other end of their journey might claim their letter is a forgery." He frowned, shaking his head. "Sir, once word spreads, we're finished."

Matthew leaned back, his head slowly bobbing, giving Damase hope his point might have finally gotten through. "I never thought of that." He stared at Damase. "What do you propose we do?"

Damase shook his head. "I'm not sure. The only pattern we've noticed is that they are using commanderies and outposts around Paris to redeem their Letters of Credit. I suggest we start there."

"How?"

"I plan on interviewing our men at each of these locations, and see if they recall any of these redemptions. We might just get lucky." He pulled out a piece of paper from his bag. "Also, I have a directive here I'd like sent out to all the locations in question, with your permission, of course." He handed over the page and Matthew read it.

"You really think this might help?"

"Every little bit of information we can gather could lead us to whoever is behind this."

Matthew handed back the directive. "It seems like a long shot."

Damase agreed. "Unfortunately, right now, that might be all we have." He held up the page. "And please make sure the directive goes out worded exactly as I have it. No one must know why they're being asked to do what I've indicated. We can't risk word spreading, even among our own. The stakes are far too high."

"Very well. I'll have it sent immediately. We have to put a stop to this before word gets out. Use as many men and resources as you need."

Damase shook his head. "No, I'll do this alone."

Matthew wagged a finger. "No, this is too important for only one person to be working on it. We need this resolved quickly."

Damase suppressed a frown, and knew arguing would be of little use. Matthew appeared firm on the matter. "Very well, though I can think of only one person I trust with this matter."

"And that is?"

"Sir Marcus de Rancourt."

Matthew smiled. "I had a feeling you'd ask for him." He snapped his fingers, and a young boy emerged from the shadows. "Get me a messenger."

"Right away, sir."

The Swan Tavern
Paris, Kingdom of France

"She-she really s-said that?"

Thomas Durant nodded vigorously. "She did indeed. She said she felt you weren't being given the respect you deserved."

Alain smiled at the contents of his cup, as if he dared not look Thomas in the eye lest he realize it was all a lie. "She-she always seemed like a n-nice lady."

I guess we're both lying now.

Getting Alain to come with them after they intercepted him stumbling home hadn't been difficult. Enzo's long shadow in the moonlight was usually enough to convince even the bravest of souls to comply with any requests made of them.

Though with Alain as inebriated as he was, Thomas had a feeling it was the offer of free drinks, rather than the fear of Enzo, that had him agreeing. Thomas had never directly dealt with Alain, their employers both in the same business though rarely mixing. He knew him from the neighborhood, of course, both having spent most of their lives within a couple of miles of this very spot.

They weren't friends, though knew each other by name, and might be considered casual acquaintances if their employers weren't rivals. And with Alain's awkward, insecure manner, not the least of which was caused by his unfortunate stutter, guilt racked Thomas with what he was doing, the shy Alain eating up everything fed him, the poor soul desperate for validation and friendship.

Thomas smiled at him. "I'm glad you realize that fact. She is, especially to those that work for her."

"Like you."

"Exactly." He jerked a thumb at Enzo, finishing yet another drink. "Even he's nice once you get to know him."

Alain glanced at the half-man half-beast out of the corner of his eye. "I s-suppose."

Thomas leaned closer, lowering his voice so no one else in this house of ill repute could hear. "My mistress tells me that you are moving up in the organization. Is she mistaken?"

Alain's eyes darted to the floor, the statement evidently as false as Thomas knew it was. Alain was the butt of every joke in Hamon Pequin's organization, and was never shown any respect. The very idea that he was moving up in the organization was inconceivable.

Yet it was a calculated question, designed to elicit a specific response.

"I take it you are hesitant to confirm this because it might betray your current master." Thomas pushed a few coins across the table. "An advance on your salary, should you choose to come work with us, eventually an equal to Enzo if you prove your loyalty."

Alain's eyes bulged at the generous sum. He quickly pocketed it then grabbed his drink, downing half. "Your-your mistress is cor-correct. I *am* moving up."

Thomas suppressed a smile. If Pequin was involved in something big, as Simone suspected, then a man like Alain would want to make his prospective employer think he was important enough to be involved. If he had even an inkling of what was going on, he'd reveal it now to impress his new "friends." "She's rarely wrong. Can you tell me what your latest responsibilities are?"

"I'm one of just a few-few that have been entrusted to…" His voice drifted off. "I-I shouldn't say."

"It's fine. You're among friends. No one will know. And besides, what could we possibly do with the information? Pequin is too big to hurt."

Alain's head slowly bobbed, his eyes bloodshot, his lower lip drooping slightly as the barmaid returned with another round, taking Thomas' almost full cup away with a slight smile, fully aware something underhanded was afoot. "Y-you're right, of course. It doesn't real-really matter." He leaned closer, his elbows slamming onto the table causing everything to bounce. "S-sorry." He beckoned them closer. "I'm involved in something b-big. You know René Courvat?"

Thomas nodded. "I do."

"Well, he-he's cracked it."

Thomas' heart thumped harder. With the mention of René's name, whatever it was they were about to hear was what they were looking for. René had paid off his loan far too fast, which meant he had more money than he should.

Just like Pequin.

"Cracked what?"

"The Temp-Templar code."

Enclos du Temple, Templar Fortress
Paris, Kingdom of France

Sir Damase sipped the strong *tisane*, made just the way he liked it—hot and full of flavor. Tepidness was never welcome in his life, whether it was in his drinks or his desire to serve. Commitment was key in both pleasure and work. He had noticed the first discrepancy. He could have let it go, but he didn't. He could no longer serve on the battlefield, the ultimate goal of any warrior monk, though he could still serve and serve honorably.

And the very idea that someone was stealing from the Order had enraged him.

Then, when he realized how they were doing it, it terrified him.

The Order was all he knew. He had grown up within it, his father a nobleman and knight who had given up everything to join the fight against the heathen Saracens. And when he was of age, he too had worked his way through the ranks, eventually becoming a knight and serving beside his father until his death in battle.

It was how he had hoped to go, but unfortunately, the Saracen that had finally put him out of commission was less skilled than the one that had felled his father. He had survived his combat-ending wound, relegated to a desk job in Rome. Though at least he was still serving.

He took another sip of his drink then resumed examining the map of Paris and surrounds, the first one he had seen of the area. He was eager to get underway, though his orders were to await Marcus' arrival, and he wasn't one to disobey orders unless he felt they were egregiously wrong—something that did happen from time to time, though never, to date, off the battlefield.

He carefully noted the locations of each of the flagged transactions, the ring around Paris confirmed. But how did that help him? Knowing the locations of the forged redemptions meant nothing due to the very nature of the Letters of Credit. As long as one knew the name it was meant for, one could redeem them. Yes, he might get lucky and have someone remember one or perhaps even several of the questionable transactions, though he doubted it. There were simply too many.

And even if they did, how could he possibly track them down? All used different names, so all were obviously fake. There was no one to look for.

He stared at the pages. The more recent transactions much larger than those that started several months ago, and more frequent. Whoever it was, they were getting greedy. His heart skipped a beat as he noticed something he hadn't before. He leaned closer.

Could it be?

He removed all the markers from the map and began anew, this time with an eye to what he had just noticed, his heart picking up speed as he realized his observation was correct. And it just might lead him somewhere.

But only if he acted fast.

And disobeyed orders.

Sevres, Kingdom of France

René bundled himself against the morning chill, using his horse as a break against the wind, the beast borrowed from an extremely guilty Mr. Fromont, responsible for revealing his secret to Pequin. Yet he didn't blame him for his current predicament.

He had been stupid. He should have kept it to himself. He shouldn't have helped anyone, at least not the way he had. By giving them the forged Letters of Credit, requiring them to go to the Templar outposts to redeem them, he had revealed the fact he had broken the code. Now, in retrospect, he knew he should have redeemed the forgeries himself, and given the money over without anyone the wiser.

Hindsight always trumped foresight, and now here he was, in the service of a cretin who would get him killed.

That was why he had hatched a plan, a plan so risky, it could mean his death, but should it work, it would mean freedom for him and his sisters. Today, he was beginning a round of redemptions, larger than any he had done before—at least personally.

Pequin had forced him to create forgeries for much larger amounts, with the redemptions completed by people under his employ, and none had been caught yet. It enraged him every time he handed over another set of falsified Letters of Credit. Why should that bastard get all the profit from what was *his* scheme and *his* neck?

This was all about to come tumbling down around

them, for there was no way the Templars wouldn't catch on eventually. And when they did, he'd be hanged, and he had to leave a legacy for his sisters, or find them husbands. Unfortunately, most of the men he knew were already happily married, and the few that weren't were men he'd never wish upon his sisters—there was a reason they weren't married. He needed to find young men for his sisters, but he knew few, the fact he was awkwardly intelligent leaving him with few friends, and even fewer peers.

His worry for his sisters, especially Grace, had forced him into a corner there was only one way out of. One last, big score. He had twelve forged Letters of Credit in his saddlebag, and would make a circuit around the city over the next few days, redeeming the largest letters of credit he ever had, and once done, he would have enough money to take him and his sisters away from the only home they had known, and up north where they had family that might take them in until he could get back on his feet.

Paris was filled with scum and villainy, and he was sick of it. Yes, his current situation was brought on by his own actions, though they were actions he was driven to because of his own desperation, and those of his neighbors. They were all victims here. Him, his sisters, the neighbors he had helped, even the Templars in a way, for it was them he was stealing from. The only one in the mix who was a true villain was Pequin, and one day the Good Lord would deliver him his due, whether in this life or the next.

Though that provided him with small comfort at this very moment, for Pequin wouldn't hesitate to kill him if the man knew what he was up to at this moment, putting the entire scheme at risk for his own purposes.

He entered the first outpost on his loop, his pulse pounding, his forehead dripping, his entire being growing faint. He paused, beginning to turn around as second thoughts overwhelmed him.

"Can I help you?"

He cursed.

To himself.

He held up his Letter of Credit. "I hope so."

De Rancourt Residence
Crécy-la-Chapelle, Kingdom of France

Lady Joanne made a point of sniffing the air. "I see you bathed."

Beatrice doled out a spoonful of porridge to Sir Marcus. "It smells like you did, anyway."

Jacques and Angeline giggled, as did young Pierre, the children sitting along one side of the table in the farmhouse, Lady Joanne and Beatrice the other, with Marcus at the head. It was a ritual Joanne insisted on whenever possible.

A family meal.

"The children need a father figure," she had said when she laid down her new "rules."

"I'm not their father, I'm their uncle."

"It doesn't matter. You're the head of the household, the man of the house, and they need that authority figure in their lives. It shows them that you want to be part of this family, that you love them, and that you will be there when they need you."

He thought the notion a little ridiculous, though he had complied. He'd much rather be eating with his men in the barracks they had built, but part of him understood what she was saying, especially when he'd walk in at mealtime and see the excited looks on the faces of the children.

He supposed he loved them. He certainly cared for them, and would die to protect them, even Pierre, who was no relation to him—he was a Templar Knight and would do that for any innocent. Yet he did miss them when he was gone, finding himself looking forward to seeing them after a long journey.

Is that love?

He honestly couldn't say. He had never loved a woman, and these past months were his first exposure to children. He had loved his parents and sister, though that was the way things were supposed to be, and having not seen them in decades, perhaps he truly had no concept of the notion.

In time, hopefully.

He waited for Beatrice to finish serving everyone, then they all joined hands, thanking the Lord for His bounty, before tucking in.

"How much longer will you be working on Pevra's barn?" asked Joanne.

"Not much. The neighbors are really pitching in, so the work is going quickly."

"I hear they weren't so eager until you laid down the law," said Beatrice.

Marcus smiled slightly. "I merely gave them the structure they so desperately needed. One hour per day from each farm's eldest son. It was enough to get the debris cleared in a couple of days, and now the lumber has been milled at cost, with most of the trees donated. We'll have it up in no time."

Joanne put down her spoon. "Good. They're decent people and didn't deserve this."

"Nobody does."

She frowned. "I can think of a few I might turn a blind eye to should something befall them."

Marcus regarded her. "That's not very Christian of

you."

Angeline's jaw dropped, Joanne noticing. "Eat your food."

"Yes, Milady." She hunkered down over her porridge, her cheeks flushed, her eyes still on the adults.

"If you act Christian, then I'll be Christian back at you. But if all you do is leech off your neighbors, never helping when needed, then no, don't expect me to come running when you're in need."

Marcus finished his porridge, leaning back, enjoying the full stomach. "Anyone in particular?"

She eyed him. "You know *exactly* who I'm talking about."

He chuckled, nodding, for he did.

A horse galloping toward the house had everyone rising. Marcus held out a hand. "Finish eating, I'll see who it is." He rose, as did his eyebrows when he spotted through the window a Templar messenger dismounting. He opened the door, the young man rushing forward and bowing.

"Are you Sir Marcus de Rancourt?"

"I am."

A folded paper was produced. "An urgent message from the Fortress, sir."

Marcus broke the seal while the messenger waited to see if there would be a reply. He quickly scanned the page, thankful it wasn't bad news, and equally thankful the coming days would be occupied with work other than farm labor. He folded the paper back up. "Tell Sir Matthew and Sir Damase that my sergeant and I will be there before the end of the day."

"Yes, sir," replied the man, quickly writing out the

message and putting it in his saddlebag. He bowed once again. "Good day to you, Sir Marcus."

"And to you."

The young man turned his horse then sped away, the rest of Marcus' entourage jogging down the hill.

"Was that a messenger?" asked Jeremy.

"Yes. Sir Damase needs me in Paris. Sergeant, you'll accompany me."

David appeared crestfallen. "We're not to come?"

Marcus shook his head. "No, you're needed here. Hopefully, we won't be too long, though I can't be certain. Sir Damase's purpose here seems complex, so it may take some time. I'll send word if we're to be more than a few days."

"But you might need our help should something go wrong."

It was obvious David was desperate to escape the farm, likely the shit-shoveling specifically. "We'll take Tanya. She's good in a fight."

Their mastiff barked at her name, her tail wagging, as if she could sense an adventure was in her future.

Jeremy looked at her. "If I could figure out how, I'd have you shoveling the barn."

David grunted. "She'd probably do a better job of it."

"Like you—"

Marcus cut them off. "Now, children, that's enough. Prep two horses with provisions for two days, just in case."

David nodded. "Yes, sir." He grabbed Jeremy and they both headed back up the hill.

Simon glanced at the farmhouse. "The Lady isn't

going to be happy."

Marcus frowned. "No, but we're Templars first, farmers second. Our agreement with Command is that Templar business supersedes our new situation."

Simon grinned. "Thank God!"

Marcus chuckled. "You may find what we're about to embark upon quite boring, my friend. I have a feeling we'll be reading more documents than we've seen in a lifetime, rather than engaging in battle."

Simon chewed his cheek for a moment. "I think I'd rather shovel shit."

Marcus laughed. "Don't let the squires hear that. One of them might just insist on taking your place."

Simon looked at Tanya. "What do you think I should do?"

Tanya barked, jumping up on her hind legs, placing her front paws on Simon's chest.

"Yes, you're right. Reading is better than shoveling." He turned to Marcus. "We're in."

Marcus eyed him. "I'm so glad you two have come to a decision together."

"There was much debate."

"I can see that. I wonder, however, if two minds were at work, or if you just share one brain."

Simon barked at him, and the children in the doorway squealed in delight, joining in along with Tanya.

Joanne stood, her hands on her hips, shaking her head. "Now you see what you've done? It'll take me all day to get them to stop."

Simon grinned. "Then it's a good thing we're leaving."

Joanne glared at him before she turned her fury toward Marcus. "Just what is he on about?"

Simon winked then bolted up the hill, leaving Marcus to break the news.

Hopefully, this drags on for a little while. It might take her more than a few days to calm down.

Thibault Residence
Paris, Kingdom of France

"Frankly, it's unbelievable!"

Simone shook her head at what Thomas had just explained to her, Enzo backing up the story told them late last night with the occasional grunt. "It is that. We need to take advantage of this. Imagine! Stealing from those holier than thou monks. They take an oath of poverty, yet are richer than kings!"

Thomas felt obligated to jump to the defense of the Templars, the few he knew personally nothing but honorable men, and certainly not wealthy. "The Order is, ma'am, not the individuals."

Simone spat. "Semantics! We need to figure out how to get in on this."

Enzo cleared his throat. "Why not just go see René and make him?"

Simone's head slowly bobbed. "We could, but with Pequin involved, that could be dangerous. He's ruthless." She looked at Thomas. "If you thought *I* had no heart, little one, you'd be gutted to find out how depraved that one is. There is a special place in Hell reserved for men like that."

Thomas' eyes bulged. "You believe in such things?"

She stared at him. "Of course I do! I'm a good Christian!"

Thomas' eyes widened further. "But, but…"

"But what?"

He stared at the floor, suddenly very uncomfortable.

"Umm, nothing."

She reached forward, tilting up his chin. "You think I'm evil? That I'm going to burn in Hell for all of eternity under the torments of Satan himself?"

He did, though he dared not answer.

She stared at him, her arms folded, accentuating the bust she used to weaken the will of the men she had dealings with. "You do, don't you? Answer me."

His heart pulsed at her demand, and he looked away again. "Well, umm, your line of work isn't, umm, exactly, umm, well…"

"Christian?"

He shrugged.

"Honest?"

He shrugged again.

She shook her head, a frown creasing her face. "You truly are a naïve boy. Don't you see that I provide a service to this community? Don't you see that I am doing the work of the Lord?"

Thomas' eyes outright bulged, his mouth agape, unable to hold his tongue. "Y-you actually believe that?"

She laughed, tossing her head back. "My boy, I don't *believe* it. I *know* it!" She leaned closer. "Think about it. When someone needs money, they come to me. I provide it to them. This allows them to fulfill their need. They then pay me back when they can."

"With interest! And penalties should they be late!" He nodded toward Enzo. "Or worse."

"Of course! Even our Lord would agree that if a promise is made, it should be kept. And I ask for nothing more than what our Lord would ask."

Thomas shook his head, dropping into his chair, flabbergasted at the gall on display.

Is she seriously comparing herself to our Lord?

"You still don't see it, do you?"

Thomas threw his hands up in the air. "Of course I don't! You have so much money compared to those you lend to. If you were truly doing the Lord's work, then why not simply give them the money, or if you must lend it to them, do so interest-free?"

She laughed, exchanging glances with a grinning Enzo. "My boy, how do you think I got so much money? It wasn't by being a charity. That's what the Church is for. No, I worked hard, and yes, charged interest on the loans I provided. But don't you see? By charging interest, it gave me more money to lend, which then let me help more people. And the interest I charged those people made me even more money, giving me even more to lend to others and help them." She sat across from him, staring into his eyes. "Need is a beast that must be continually fed, and I am a fulfiller of need, charging a fee that allows me to fulfill the ever-growing need." She jabbed a finger at him. "And I am much more kind about it than most in my business, like that cutthroat Pequin. Have you ever known me to kill someone who owes me money?"

Thomas hadn't, though that didn't make her an angel. "No, and God help us all if you ever did. But you've had them beaten, their bones broken, and whatnot. You're not exactly a gentle soul."

She chuckled. "True. But that's all part of doing business. No one must ever think they can borrow from me and not fulfill their obligations. If word were to spread that I might let them get away with it without a toll being exacted, no one would pay me. Enzo here is saving lives by delivering messages not only to a delinquent debtor, but to all those who might think of becoming delinquent themselves." She sighed, shaking her head. "In time, little one, you'll come to see that what I do is necessary, and a community service. Am I really that different than your local priest who demands you fill his collection basket with money you don't have in order to gain entry into Heaven? Forcing the poor to subsidize the Roman Catholic Church, now that's thievery. I let my debtors keep their money, and only pay me the interest they owe."

Thomas grunted. "Meaning they are forever in your debt."

She grinned. "It's a brilliant business, isn't it? Interest only loans. The key to giving everyone what they want." She tapped her chin. "Now, back to the business at hand. Now that we know there is a way to beat the Templars at their own game, how do we profit from it, without actually participating?" Her eyes widened, a smile spreading as she laughed, a cackle that sent shivers up and down his spine, a shrill utterance that would have been at home among the Devil's minions in the pits of Hell where he was certain she would one day permanently reside.

"What?" he asked, terrified of what the answer might be.

She shook her head. "Oh, no, there are some things that simply cannot be shared." She stood then headed out of his office, clearly pleased with herself. "This one, my boy, must be kept to myself. But it will definitely change things around here, should it work."

He looked at Enzo who shrugged. "I've learned not

to ask.”

Chaville, Kingdom of France

René stood by his horse, staring at the Templar outpost across the street. His entire body trembled, his back soaked with fear, as he closed his eyes, willing himself to calm down.

Yet it was impossible.

He should never have gone into that first outpost, yet he had. And the change in procedure was immediately noticed, though only because he had done this so many times, he knew the routine so well. The clerk that had served him had taken notes, the man's eyes darting from him to the page and back.

Though that wasn't all.

It was the notches on the door, each with a symbol beside it that he knew from having broken the code were numbers. Sequential. He had wondered what they were for, and it wasn't until he was well out of town that he realized exactly what was going on. The clerk had been taking notes about *him*, and those notches and their corresponding numbers were to tell the clerk how tall he was.

It was ingenious.

And terrifying.

It meant that his secret had been discovered. These changes in procedure had to be because the Order had figured out someone was manipulating their system. Yet the fact he had walked out, unscathed, suggested they had no idea who that someone might be. But it also meant they would soon have his description once they reconciled his forged letters of credit with the recorded details should he continue. Once they did figure out the similarities, the Templar fortress in Paris would no doubt send his description to every outpost in the area, and the next time he redeemed a Letter of Credit, he'd be flagged and scrutinized in earnest.

He'd be done for.

He sighed. And that meant only one thing. If he wanted to save his sisters from Pequin, he had to commit now, before it was too late. He pulled the next Letter of Credit from his saddlebag and squared his shoulders as he took a deep breath.

Courage, René, courage.

Chaville, Kingdom of France

"What's he doing?"

Lyon shrugged. "I don't know, but he's not on a run for us. The boss said he could redeem one a week for himself, but this is the second time today."

Alain watched as René disappeared inside the Templar outpost. "Should we st-stop him?"

Lyon shook his head slowly. "I don't know. Maybe he *is* on a run for the boss, and we weren't told."

"But-but what if he isn't? The boss will be p-pissed if we let him get away with whatever he's doing."

Lyon chewed his cheek, staring at the now closed door of the outpost. "But if we stop him, and the boss sent him, he'll slit our throats."

Alain's chest tightened and his stomach flipped at the thought of an angry Pequin. The man was terrifying at the best of times, which was why he had foolishly had drinks with Thomas and Enzo. His memory was fuzzy, and he feared he might have said too much, though there had been no consequences—so far.

And no further offer of employment.

That fact had him curious. Had it all been a ruse? And if so, to what end? He had talked, but he wasn't sure what he had said. He had a vague recollection of talking about René, though he was sure he wouldn't have been that stupid.

Talk like that could get him killed.

It had to have been a dream.

No one crossed Pequin.

Not if they wanted to live.

"Umm, maybe we should find out?"

Lyon nodded. "Good idea. You go back to Paris and find out what the boss wants us to do."

Alain's eyes narrowed. "But I-I won't be back until to-tomorrow! How will I find you?"

"Just follow the route. I'll leave a message at the local tavern closest to the Templar outpost to let you know I've been there."

Alain frowned. "But that c-could waste a lot of time."

Lyon smacked the back of Alain's head. "Use your head for once! Make a guess as to where you think we'll be by tomorrow, then head there. If there's no message, then you know I haven't arrived yet, so just wait. If there is, then you know to continue on. You'll catch up soon enough."

Alain rubbed the back of his head, always hating it when Lyon hit him like that. "Wh-what if he doesn't fol-follow the route?"

"Then head home."

"Umm, h-how long should I wait?"

Another smack left Alain wincing with the shame. "If you pick a town no more than a day's ride from here, and we don't reach it by end of day tomorrow, then you know something went wrong. Just head back and let the boss know. Chances are I'll already be there."

"Oh, I get it."

Lyon shook his head, sighing. "You're so stupid, sometimes I wonder if your mother bred with one of the farm animals and not your father."

Rage inflamed his stomach. "That's disgusting."

Lyon gestured toward the horses. "You're an idiot. Now get going before you get lost in the dark, imbecile."

Alain said nothing, instead mounting his horse and heading back toward Paris, his stomach in knots, his chest tight, his eyes burning with the tears he so desperately wanted to shed. He was stupid compared to the others. He knew it. And there was nothing he could do about it. He couldn't read or write, though few of the crew could. But even simple words, like a sign on a building, were beyond him. Everything simply appeared as a jumble of letters. He could look at the same sign every day and it would never read the same to him.

Even his eyes were stupid.

And his stutter was a constant source of delight for those supposed to be his friends. He had been afflicted with it his entire life, or at least as long as he could remember. His mother told him he didn't stutter as a child, and that if he put his mind to it, he'd overcome it, though no matter how hard he tried, it was of no use.

He was too stupid to speak normally.

You're an imbecile, just like he said.

Just like they all *say.*

He sighed, the tears finally flowing as he cleared the outskirts of the town, at last alone with his thoughts.

But you're strong.

It was true. While he might be colossally stupid, he was the strongest man he knew. It was why Pequin kept him around. If muscle was needed, if speed was needed, he could run down a man and lay a beating on him like no one's business.

Even two or three good men couldn't stop him.

His record was eight, though in their defense, three were so drunk they could barely stand, but five of them put up a good fight. It had been a great night, his stutter and broken mind forgotten by his comrades as they toasted his feat.

Yet it was soon forgotten, and within days he was the idiot who had lost his village.

He leaned forward in his saddle, urging his horse onward to Paris, hoping to beat the sun's dip below the horizon.

Enclos du Temple, Templar Fortress
Paris, Kingdom of France

"I'm afraid he left already."

Marcus eyed the man at the front desk of the Templar Headquarters for the Kingdom of France. "But only this morning I received an urgent message to come here and join him."

"Yes, sir. Your message was sent late yesterday." He riffled through a pile of papers before finding what he was looking for. He handed it over. "Sir Damase left this for you."

Marcus cracked the seal then unfolded the page, his eyebrows rising with the lengthy instructions on how to find Damase. "Is he serious with this?"

"I'm sure I don't know, sir, though he did hand it to me with a straight face."

"Of course he did." He sighed. "Fine. We'll need provisions for two men and a dog for two days. We'll resupply at one of our outposts should it become necessary. And two fresh horses."

The man snapped his fingers and a boy emerged from the shadows. "You heard Sir Marcus' requirements?"

The boy nodded.

"Then see to them at once."

The boy bowed then sped off, nearly running headlong into Sir Matthew Norris.

Marcus and Simon both bowed to the most senior member of their order in the Kingdom. "Sir Matthew, an honor."

Matthew acknowledged them. "I would speak with you, Sir Marcus."

Marcus hesitated. "And my sergeant?"

Matthew eyed Simon for a moment. "Do you keep any secrets from him?"

"None."

"Then I see no point in you having to repeat my words to him." He spun on his heel and they followed, Simon flashing a toothy grin at Marcus. Simon closed the door to Matthew's office, and they both waited for him to sit.

"How may we be of service, sir?"

Matthew didn't appear pleased, his face stern, his knuckles white as his hands clenched the arms of his chair. "Sir Damase left without my blessing. I ordered him to wait for you, yet he rushed off without telling me."

Marcus shifted in his chair, tempering his desire to leap to his friend's defense. "I'm certain he had his reasons. He's a good man, and loyal to the Order. For him to ignore an order from you, well…"

"I agree. I think he figured out a way to catch whoever is behind this, and decided he couldn't wait." He pursed his lips, staring at Marcus then Simon for a moment. "I also fear he doesn't trust anyone but you."

"Surely he trusts you, sir."

Matthew grunted. "I would hope so, though I wouldn't blame him if he didn't. If he's right about what he's found—"

"You have doubts?"

Matthew sighed. "I did at first, but the evidence he

brought is quite compelling. And the implications are significant. If he is right, and I fear he is, and someone has broken our code, it could be a serious blow to the Order. If word were to get out, our entire communications system, and our Letters of Credit, could be called into question. This must be stopped before anyone finds out."

Marcus nodded. "Agreed. We can't have anyone out there who knows our code." He pursed his lips. "Which begs the question, sir, what do we do if we find whoever is behind this?"

Matthew sighed, leaning back. "I too have been troubled by this question. He will have to be interrogated, of course. We must know if he has told anyone of his discovery. If we're lucky, it's a lone man who has told no one. But if he has, we must know. If this knowledge has been shared, then we must track down every single person that has been exposed."

"Then do what?"

"Kill them."

Marcus' chest tightened. "Really? Must it come to that? What about justice?"

"In this case, justice will be delivered by us, rather than the King and his court." Matthew shook his head. "If he catches wind, it could be trouble for us. Which is why this must be handled *very* quietly. Beyond the three of us and Damase, only two others know, and they are in Rome. I trust our people to keep the secret, but men arrested and handed over to the court will reveal what they know, and even if ultimately put to death for the theft of our money, all will know that the code has been broken." He sighed. "No, I'm afraid we must deal with this ourselves. The risk to the Order is too great."

Marcus exchanged an uncomfortable glance with Simon. "Do we have the Pope's blessing?"

"Sir Damase brought a letter with him from His Holiness, giving me broad discretion in all matters with respect to the continued security of the Order."

Marcus regarded hiim. "That sounds rather ambiguous, sir. Does he know the specifics?"

Matthew shook his head. "No. It was apparently decided by my counterpart in Rome that no one outside the Order, including His Holiness, should know. I assume he was told of an important security issue that His Holiness not being privy to was best, and the dispensation was granted."

"King Philip won't be happy if he finds out the Pope granted us such powers."

Matthew agreed. "No, he won't. Which is another reason why this must be dealt with swiftly and discreetly, otherwise the Order we hold so dear could collapse."

Simon leaned forward. "Do you really think it could come to that?"

Matthew nodded. "I do. Imagine if the royal families and the noble families decided we could no longer be trusted with their wealth? They could pull all of their funds at once, and our system would collapse. So much of it is invested in property and other holdings now, that we would be forced to sell to cover the withdrawals. The entire system could collapse, and with it, the Order. Should kings lose their fortunes, or their faith in us, pressure would be put on Rome for our endorsement by the Pope to be revoked, and we would be nothing. Finished. And it could happen within a matter of months, if not weeks."

"But the system is needed! What will the pilgrims do? It will be open season on them if they're forced to carry their valuables with them."

Matthew sighed. "I have little doubt, in time, someone else will fill the void left by us."

Marcus frowned. "You mean the Hospitallers."

Simon spat on the floor, immediately apologizing. "Sorry, sirs. Force of habit."

Matthew chuckled. "No need to apologize, Sergeant, I feel the same way. The rivalry between our two orders is old, and I fear will last long after I'm dead and gone. Why we can't peacefully coexist is beyond me, but I fear jealousy is a cruel mistress. You know, I actually met their grand prior a few years ago, and he accused me, he accused all of us, of being bad Christians, because of our wealth? It was everything I could do to not run him through on the spot."

Marcus smiled. "It's probably for the best that you were able to control yourself, sir."

"Probably, though it would have felt good." Matthew sighed. "Can you imagine if someone like them were to find out about this? There would be nothing we could do to stop them from destroying us once and for all."

A knock at the door halted the conversation. "Yes?" called Matthew.

The door opened and the young boy from earlier entered, bowing deeply. "Sir, the requested horses and provisions for Sir Marcus are ready."

Matthew dismissed the boy with a flick of the wrist and he slunk back through the door, closing it behind him. Matthew rose, as did Marcus and Simon. "I wish you success, Sir Marcus. I shall be praying for it tonight." He glanced out the window at the setting sun. "Will you be staying with us tonight, or striking out now?"

Marcus shook his head. "Neither. I have a letter to deliver from one young lover to another, and hope to take advantage of his hospitality before we leave tomorrow morning. It would be foolish even for Templars to ride at night in this area."

"I could assign an escort."

Marcus dismissed the offer. "An escort demands questions be asked and suspicions may arise. Let us keep this operation contained to the few of us. We will rendezvous with Damase by noon tomorrow, and hopefully he will have some news as to why he disobeyed your orders."

Matthew nodded. "I'm eager to hear his explanation. Hopefully it satisfies me, otherwise I might have to exercise my new powers granted by Rome in this matter."

Marcus stared at him, his eyes flaring for but a moment. A smile crept up the corners of Matthew's mouth.

"We must work on that sense of humor, Sir Marcus, otherwise you may be mistaken into thinking I'm more of the tyrant than I am."

Simon punched Marcus in the shoulder. "I got it." He bowed slightly at Matthew. "Very good one, sir."

Marcus shook his head. "I must no longer be used to subtle humor, sir, as I am surrounded by wit wielded with the delicacy of a hammer."

Matthew laughed, waving them toward the door. "Ahh, the comradery of soldiers. How I miss it! Now go, so you can deliver your message and be up all the earlier tomorrow. Put a stop to this, Sir Marcus, for all our sakes."

"I shall do my best, sir."

Marcus left the office, Simon on his heels, and they headed outside, their fresh horses waiting in what remained of the sunlight, the long shadows cast by the low sun stretched across the courtyard. They mounted and Simon turned to his master.

"To Thomas'?"

Marcus nodded. "To Thomas'. Let's hope he doesn't mind the company."

"We could always return here if necessary."

Marcus urged his horse forward, sighing as they passed through the gates. "No, I would rather ride through the night should it be necessary. I fear sleeping here might remind me too much of what I've been missing, and I may never return to the farm."

Simon regarded him. "Really? You would consider not returning?"

Marcus frowned, shaking his head. "I would hope not, but every time I see our brothers in such numbers, I ache for the old days." He growled. "It is selfish of me, I know. My new responsibilities—"

"—*our* new responsibilities—"

Marcus acquiesced. "You are right, of course, *our* new responsibilities, are just as important as anything we have done in our decades of service, but I can honestly say, with the shame these words are due, that if I had received word that my sister had died before we left the Holy Land, I fear I wouldn't have come. I would have left those poor children to the Church and never given it a second thought."

Simon smiled gently. "My friend, I've known you

for over twenty years, and I can with confidence say that almost every word you just said there is bullshit."

Marcus' eyes shot wide and he turned toward his oldest and closest friend. "Oh?" His eyes narrowed. "You said *almost* every word. Which of mine rung true?"

"That our new responsibilities are just as important as anything we've done. And the man I know, the man I have sworn to serve all these years, would never leave his nephew and niece to fend for themselves, even if the gentle hands of the Church were involved. If you had known she had died, and that those children were alone, you would have been here all the quicker, and I would have been there with you, along with David and Jeremy. Never doubt that your heart is as good as any man's. Better! Don't let nostalgia brought on by crisp white tunics and bold red crosses cause you to question what might have been."

Marcus' chest ached at the words delivered in earnest by the truest friend he had ever known. "You are a good friend." He reached out and grabbed Simon by the shoulder. "I'm happy you chose to stay with me. Without you and the others, I know I would not have been up to the challenge."

"Nonsense. You would have succeeded brilliantly, I'm sure."

Marcus grunted. "Now you flatter me."

"More nonsense. If I were to flatter you, I'd tell you that you were the most handsome man I had ever met, and that the men of this wretched city are fortunate you entered the Order and took a vow of celibacy, otherwise their wives and daughters wouldn't be safe."

Marcus shook his head, chuckling. "I sometimes wonder about you, my friend."

"I should hope you're always wondering."

Marcus tossed his head back, laughing heartily. "Too true!" He smiled, regarding his friend. "It would be a boring life without you and the squires. I thank God every day that He brought you into my life." He pursed his lips. "Perhaps it is you and the others that made life in the Order so enjoyable. A life of sacrifice, devoted to our Lord, never seemed tedious or hard, as long as I knew you and the others would always be there at the end of the day when our prayers and duties were done."

Simon nodded ahead as they rounded the last bend leading to Thomas Durant's humble home, left to him by his murdered father only last year. "Last chance to change your mind."

Marcus shook his head. "No, we shall stay with Master Thomas, or ride. The comradery I seek is already at my side and ahead of me. Dwelling on the past is of no value. We have new lives now, as honorable as any, and as fulfilling as any."

Simon grinned. "Agreed. We shovel shit by day, and get ordered about by women at night. I can't imagine a better life."

Marcus laughed. "Nor can I!"

St. Denis, Kingdom of France

Sir Damase dismounted and stretched. It had been a hard ride from Paris, and his old bones were feeling it. He patted his horse, the mare having done a good job of getting him here quickly.

For time was of the essence. After finally seeing a map of Paris and its surrounds, and examining the logs of the transactions in question, he had noticed a pattern. Not only were the redemptions always in towns surrounding the outskirts of Paris, as he already knew, those that were done in bunches spanning a few days were done in a loop, starting in the northwest, and circling the city counterclockwise.

Every time.

It was the first repeated pattern he had seen, and St. Denis was where they always finished.

Yet he had little hope of catching the person responsible, as he still had no idea who to look for. Every transaction had used a different name and a different amount, but these more recent transactions, the larger ones where greed appeared to have entered the picture, were all in a large, sequential loop around Paris that took several days to complete.

That meant a single person, otherwise they would have broken up the task into at least batches so they could collect the funds quicker.

And a single person might mean the secret was contained.

The possibility gave him hope, and determination to bring this to an end swiftly. And with fresh records only days old at the fortress in Paris, unlike the months old records he had been examining in Rome, he had been able to compare them to the records he had brought with him, and found another set of forgeries—a circuit had been completed only days ago, all with origins in Rome, all dated before he had left, so if they were genuine, they would be in his records.

They weren't.

And that meant the transactions might still be fresh in the minds of those who had processed them.

He stepped through the door, spotting the notches in the frame he had ordered, the Templar messenger network swift and efficient, especially in close quarters such as Paris.

The knight behind the desk at the center of the entrance rose. "Good day, sir. I am Sir Gile Bonin. How may I be of service?"

Damase bowed. "I am Sir Damase de Sissey. I am here on an urgent matter from Rome, and with the blessing of Sir Matthew Norris."

Sir Gile motioned toward the chair sitting in front of his desk. "Sit, Sir Damase. How may I help?"

Damase sat, as did Gile, then pulled out a sheaf of papers, quickly finding the transaction redeemed here only days ago. He handed it to Gile. "Do you recall this transaction?"

Gile read the page, his head slowly bobbing. "Yes, I do, as a matter of fact, though only because of his stutter."

"Stutter?"

"Yes. The man could barely speak. It was really quite trying."

"What can you tell me about him?"

Gile shrugged. "Not much. About your height, your build. Perhaps twenty years old. Dark hair, if I recall. Nothing really that stood out beyond the stutter."

"Had you ever seen him before?"

Gile shook his head. "No, I think I'd remember that stutter, though I'm not the only one who works this desk. I'll ask the others when it's their shift."

"Do that. If you find anything, send a message to the fortress."

"Of course."

He retrieved another transaction, another batch all with origins in the Holy Land. "What about this one, about two weeks ago." He handed over the page. "Any recollection?"

Gile read the page, slowly shaking his head. "No, I can't say I remember this one."

He reached over, pointing at the time of the transaction. "It appears to have been quite late."

Gile's mouth opened slightly as his eyes widened. "That's right, I *do* remember this. He came in a few moments after I was supposed to close for the night. I told him to come back in the morning, but he begged me, saying his sister was ill and he needed the money. I took pity on him." He paused. "Why all the questions? Is there a problem?"

He shook his head. "Nothing to be concerned about, nothing you or this office has done wrong." He redirected the conversation. "Do you recall what he looked like? Was he the same stutterer?"

Gile shook his head. "No, definitely not the same man. This one was a little stouter, a ruddy face. Looked like a bit of a bruiser, if you ask me."

Damase rose, extending his hand. "Thank you, Sir

Gile, you've been a great help."

Gile rose, accepting the hand. "I will ask the others about both these men, and get word to you should I discover anything."

"Thank you." Damase headed for the door then stopped. He turned to face Gile. "I almost forgot. If Sir Marcus de Rancourt should arrive here, tell him I'm heading for Aubervilliers."

Gile jotted down the note. "I shall make sure he is made aware."

"Thank you." Damase left and mounted his horse, heading for the next town on the loop around Paris he had discovered. The excitement of having his first real lead was trounced by the knowledge there were two different people involved. His hope of it being one man who had broken the code, one man taking advantage of the situation to benefit himself only, was not the case.

Two meant a conspiracy.

And neither man described sounded like men who could crack a code used by the Order for well over a century, unbroken. And unfortunately, it would make it all the harder to put a stop to it if more than one was involved. For all he knew, there could be a dozen men, each running a loop only once so as to never get recognized.

That would make sense.

He pulled up on the reins, bringing his horse to a halt as he sat in his saddle, thinking. He had little doubt the next outpost would confirm his theory of a loop, each carried out by a single man. And it meant there would be no way to catch him, even if he had their descriptions put out to all outposts in the loop, if each time it was a different person.

He was wasting everyone's time.

He closed his eyes, taking a slow breath, when an idea occurred to him and a smile spread.

"Hey Templar, did you forget how to ride a horse?"

Damase opened his eyes to find two Hospitaller Knights riding toward him.

He frowned.

He didn't have time for this. He had been warned that trouble had been brewing with the Hospitallers in Paris since they established their first fortress and clinic to treat the sick, a goodwill gesture designed to put them in King Philip's good books, as it was clear the Templars were not.

"Do you need some help, little one? Are you lost?"

The man's voice was as high-pitched as any boy's.

And Damase couldn't resist.

"Challenge me when your balls have dropped, child. Perhaps then I might feel intimidated by the likes of you."

The man's jaw dropped, his eyes bulging, his companion unsuccessfully attempting to hide his own laughter.

And Damase still didn't have time for any of this.

He turned, ignoring the feeble taunts that were finally hurled at his back, instead returning to the outpost in St. Denis, composing in his head the message he needed urgently sent by Sir Gile. The next loop around the city was due to begin in a couple of days, if their previous pattern held. If he could get his message out in time, they might just put an end to this, once and for all.

Though the strain it would put on the messenger

network might give the administration in Paris pause.

Though it would be far less than the amounts yet to be stolen should the fraud continue.

Sir Gotfried's Headquarters
Paris, Kingdom of France

Simone's knee bounced uncontrollably, this the most uncomfortable she had felt in years. She hated coming here, though once a month she was forced to.

Thanks to her late husband.

It was ironic, in fact, that she should feel the way she did. It must be how her debtors felt every time they came to see her.

Nervous.

Scared.

Angry.

Her husband had taken out a loan with these people years ago. A substantial loan. A loan she would be paying off for years. When an illness had swept through the city several years back, many had died, including many of their debtors. It had left them with little working capital, and with some of those loans financed through others while her husband had expanded their little empire far too quickly, payments became due, and their cashflow had been severely crippled.

They were about to become delinquent themselves, with people who wouldn't hesitate to cause them serious injury, or worse.

So, he had borrowed from the man who now sat behind a large, ornate desk, reading something while she waited, ignored.

And this man, and those he worked for, were never to be trifled with.

Oh Lord, if he managed to make it up there, give him a smack for me, will you?

Her husband had never been a good businessman. He had tried, but she had been the brains behind the operation the entire time.

Except when he stepped out on his own, making foolish decisions based upon unbridled greed.

Too much of her profits had been servicing this debt for too long, and she prayed what she had discovered would be her ticket out of the mess.

Sir Gotfried finally looked up from his ledger, the crest of his proud order displayed behind him, his face one of quiet dignity, though as she knew only too well, ruthless when needed. She had learned long ago to never cross the man, and was convinced the beating her husband had taken at the hands of this man's underlings contributed to his death from smallpox.

"A pleasure to see you, as always, Mrs. Thibault." His smile was pleasant, though the tone indicated a subtext that kept her on edge.

She buried her nerves as best she could, returning the smile. "Likewise, I'm sure."

"And what can I do for you today? Your payment isn't due for another three days. I hope you're not here to tell me there's going to be a delay."

A lump formed in her throat. "No, there won't be. Though I think with the information I have come across, at *great* expense and risk to myself, I might add, that you'll forgive all amounts owing."

Gotfried's eyebrows rose slightly and he leaned back, folding his arms. "You have piqued my interest, Mrs. Thibault. Please explain."

She suppressed a smile, this the most engaged she

had seen the man. "What if I told you that the Templars' code has been cracked."

Gotfried's eyes shot wide for a brief moment, revealing the value of her information before he could recover his composure. "Why do I doubt a woman like you could crack a code we've been trying to figure out for over a century?"

She chuckled as she relaxed slightly, the man having revealed the value yet again. "Oh, I assure you, sir, it wasn't I that broke it, though I know who did."

"And how do you know this?"

"Because he, and others, have been using their newfound knowledge to forge Letters of Credit and successfully redeem them for months now."

Gotfried leaned forward. "And again, how do you know this?"

"Because several of my debtors have paid back what they owed me far quicker than they should have."

Gotfried grunted. "With the rates you charge, it's a wonder anyone ever pays you back."

She flashed him a grin. "That's the entire point, isn't it?"

He smiled slightly. "I suppose it is, isn't it? And you know who this man is? This forger? This code breaker?"

"I do."

"And in exchange for his name, you want your debt with us cleared?"

Her chest tightened, the moment of truth nearing. "I do."

"Very well. Give me his name and we will pick him up. If what you say is true, your husband's debt to us is paid in full. You have my word."

Her heart hammered. "I'd, umm, like that in writing."

Gotfried leaped to his feet, glaring at her. "I am a knight! That should be all the guarantee you need."

She rose, shaking, nearly soiling herself. "Of course, sir, of course." She bowed herself toward the door, hastily backing away.

"Aren't you forgetting something?"

She paused, the blood draining from her face. "I-I don't think so."

"His name!"

Her jaw slackened and her bladder threatened to release. "Oh my! I-I forgot in all the excitement." She removed a slip of paper tucked up her sleeve, and placed it on the desk. "His name is René Courvat. This is where he lives."

"Very well. You'll hear from us very soon." She was about to open the door to leave when he stopped her. "Oh, and Mrs. Thibault."

"Yes?"

"Speak of this to no one. If I find out you have told someone of our involvement, you will pay with your life."

She paled and all strength flowed out her extremities before she remembered to breathe. "I-I understand." She spun on her heel and hurried out, praying to God that what she had done was the wise move she had been certain it was only moments ago.

Durant Residence
Paris, Kingdom of France

"How's her writing coming?"

Thomas tore his eyes away from the letter delivered earlier in the evening by Marcus, a letter Marcus had noted the young man had read at least a dozen times. He blushed. "Umm, much improved. Lady Joanne is an excellent teacher."

"She is that," agreed Marcus, tossing another piece of pheasant meat to Tanya, who snapped it from the air and swallowed it whole, eagerly anticipating the next morsel. "She's even got David and Jeremy recognizing their letters now. I think before the year is out, those two could be reading and writing."

Thomas picked at his food, the young man's appetite lost somewhere this evening. "It's a shame so few give it a second thought. I thank God every day that my father had the good sense to make certain I knew how to read and write and work with numbers. If he hadn't, I don't know what I would do." He held up his arms with a wry grin. "I don't exactly have the body of a laborer."

Simon chuckled. "A few months working the farm and eating the good cooking of the women will put some meat on those bones. You'll be bulging like a dock worker in no time."

Thomas grunted, staring back at the unfolded paper containing Isabelle's love letter. "I somehow doubt it." He frowned. "She'd probably like it, though."

Marcus regarded his young friend. "And what

makes you say that?"

Thomas shrugged. "I don't know. Don't all women prefer a strong man to protect them and provide for them?"

Simon laughed. "You're asking the wrong two men. We're both sworn to celibacy."

"So, you've never been with a woman?"

Marcus shook his head. "Never."

Thomas frowned. "Me neither. I, umm, wouldn't know what to do."

"Don't worry, boy, when the time comes, you'll figure it out."

Simon made some crude finger motions. "Every man and woman on Earth have been figuring what to put where since Adam and Eve. I'm sure you'll do fine."

Thomas flushed. "I, umm, hear if you don't know what you're doing, the woman won't enjoy herself."

Simon grinned. "That's why you practice! When you get married, you two will be going at each other as if the fate of mankind depended upon it."

Thomas turned outright red. "Marriage? Oh, I don't know about that."

Marcus regarded him. "Why's that? I thought you loved this girl."

Thomas shrugged. "I do, I suppose."

"You suppose? You better be certain, boy. That girl loves you, and she certainly thinks you're going to be getting married. Break her heart, and you'll have some very angry people to deal with."

"Including me," said Simon, his growl menacing.

Thomas paled. "The last thing I want to do is hurt her!"

Marcus relaxed his tone. "Tell me what's bothering you."

"It's my work. I-I can't bring her here to be part of this life. She's too innocent. Too pure. Paris would eat her alive. This life would destroy what I love most about her."

Marcus understood the boy's concerns and agreed with his assessment. He hated Paris. It was filthy, crime-ridden, and a place he avoided whenever possible. Isabelle, having spent her entire life in the same, tiny village of Crécy-la-Chapelle, would quickly tire of the wonder of the city, and realize how harsh things truly were.

Especially with Thomas' new line of work giving him more money than most around here. Jealousy was a horrible, twisted thing, especially among those who had nothing but their misery to occupy their time.

"Then perhaps you should join us on the farm. You know the invitation still stands."

Thomas frowned then squeezed his skinny arms. "Like I said, I'm not exactly built for the farm."

Simon flexed an arm. "And as I said, after one season, you'll be as big as me."

Marcus nodded. "You should come back with us. Tell Mrs. Thibault that you appreciate everything she's done for you, but it is time for you to get married and start a family, and you want to do that where your bride-to-be lives. Come stay with us, get married, and start working on some babies."

Simon jabbed the air with his finger. "*That's* the practice I was talking about!"

Thomas flushed again, then looked about his home. "I don't know if I could leave this. It's all I have left of my parents. If I leave, it will be torn down for scrap before the first snow falls."

"Then let it. Your home is where your heart is. Your father and mother live on in your memories, not this place. They will be with you wherever you go. Just like my sister, God rest her soul, I know she's always with me, no matter where I lay my head."

Simon grunted. "Which is why we're on the farm. He knew full well that if we returned to the Holy Land and left her children to the Church, she'd haunt him until the day he died."

Marcus chuckled. "I'm sure that played some small part in my decision making. But in all seriousness, this is just a place, filled with memories, good and bad, and those memories will remain with you, no matter where you make your home. But I think I can safely say that should you come and join us on the farm, and marry the beautiful Isabelle, your future will be filled with more good memories than bad. Though should you decide to remain here, and continue in your current vocation, I fear on your deathbed the memories you will recall will be ones you would rather not take to your grave."

Thomas sighed, closing his eyes, no doubt picturing the murder of his father only months before. "You're right, of course. I do love her, and I think deep down I know this place is merely an excuse I'm using to keep myself from committing to a future I'm not sure I'm ready for."

"From what I've been told, no one is ever sure." Marcus finished the last of his stew, setting the bowl aside before wiping his mouth with the back of his hand, something Lady Joanne would have admonished him for. "Enough of this discussion. It is your decision to make, and I will pressure you no more." He lay on his side, facing the warmth of the fire. "We will ride at first light. We must rendezvous with Sir Damase as quickly as possible before the old fool gets himself killed for asking the wrong questions of the wrong person."

Thomas leaned against the wall beside the hearth. "And what Templar business has you here this time?"

Marcus propped up his head in his hand as he scratched his beard. "I'm afraid it's nothing I can share with you, lad, but it's quite serious, or rather could be. Hopefully, we'll get this all cleared up in a few days, bring the culprit or culprits to justice, then get back to the farm in time to help David and Jeremy with the spring planting."

Simon grunted. "Perhaps a few extra days in Paris might not be a bad idea."

Marcus laughed. "We'll make a farmer out of you yet."

"I somehow doubt it. My skills lie elsewhere."

"True for all of us, but we must learn to expand our horizons."

Simon folded his arms. "I find chasing code breakers and fraudsters much more entertaining than sowing seeds and tilling soil. Don't you?"

Thomas' eyebrows shot up, his eyes wide.

"What is it, boy?"

Thomas recovered slightly. "Umm, it's what Simon said about code breakers and fraudsters. Is that why you're here?"

Marcus gave Simon the stink-eye then shook his head at Thomas. "I'm afraid we can't talk about it, and you should forget what my evidently moron for a sergeant said."

Simon appeared genuinely contrite. "Sorry."

Thomas stared about the room, uncomfortable.

"What is it, boy? What's made you so nervous?"

Thomas looked everywhere but at Marcus, saying nothing.

Marcus eyed him. "Do you know something you shouldn't?"

Thomas' cheeks flushed and he finally settled on staring at his hands, wringing in his lap. "I do, if you're here because someone has broken the Templar code."

Marcus' jaw dropped and he turned toward Simon to find him equally as shocked. He regained his composure, and sat up, cross-legged. "Tell me everything you know, now."

Thomas stared at him, his eyes filled with tears, his shoulders trembling. "But if I do, they'll kill me for sure!"

The Shrieking Owl Tavern
Paris, Kingdom of France

Alain leaped from his horse and entered the tavern, heading for the rear where Pequin always set up shop at this time of night. Those with problems would line up to see him, and Pequin would solve those problems.

For a price.

He was a terrifying man, and unforgiving when it came to debts owed, which to Alain clearly illustrated how desperate these poor souls were to enter into an agreement with a man so evil. Yet their desperation kept him employed, something he was truly grateful for, no matter how much he feared his boss.

He pushed his way through the crowd, and when Pequin spotted him, he nearly soiled his trousers at the look.

"Where the hell have you been? You were supposed to report in hours ago."

"I-I'm sorry, boss, but he left t-town, so we had to follow him. There-there was no time to let anyone know."

Pequin's eyes narrowed. "Who left town? René?"

Alain nodded vigorously, hoping to shift Pequin's ire to someone else. "Yes, he's doing the-the loop! He's going to the T-Templar outposts and re-redeeming Letters of Credit."

"And you didn't stop him?"

Alain paled. "We-we weren't sure if he was doing it for him-himself or for you. I mean, who-who would have thought the bastard would have the b-balls to cross you?"

Pequin growled, regarding him for a moment before sighing heavily. "I certainly wouldn't have." Alain visibly relaxed. "So, where's Lyon? I assume he's still with him?"

"Yes, sir. I c-came on my own to let you know what's going on, and to f-find out what you want us to do. I'll m-meet up with him tomorrow. He's g-going to leave messages in each t-town he visits."

"Good thinking."

Alain smiled, but said nothing, too scared he might say the wrong thing and send Pequin into another foul mood. Pequin scratched his crotch then took a drink.

"Everything is set for this weekend's run?"

"Yes, sir. René g-gave us the p-papers yesterday."

Pequin pursed his lips, thinking. "If he's doing a run on his own, then either he knows something we don't, or he's planning on running." He scratched again. "Pick up his sisters. Tonight." He pointed at Alain. "And you go meet up with Lyon and follow René. Let him finish the run."

"Sir?"

Pequin shrugged. "We might as well. When he returns for his sisters, we'll take the money, and lock him in a cold dark place where he can keep working for us until I tire of him."

Alain grinned. "G-good thinking, sir. We thought you'd just w-want to kill him. This is-is much better."

Pequin grunted. "That's why I'm the boss, and you fools aren't." He pounded the table, its contents rattling. "Now, get to work. I want his sisters secured within the hour." He raised a hand. "And don't lay a finger on them. They're mine."

Alain grinned. "You're a lucky m-man, boss."

Pequin laughed. "This job does have its perks!"

The others roared dutifully with laughter, and Alain slunk away, his smile fading as he wondered if the lecherous example of humanity intended to have his way with the oldest sister, or the youngest.

Or both.

He shuddered at the thought.

He mounted his horse, heading for his rented room, intent on getting a good night's sleep before he headed out in the morning, there being little point in traveling in the dark. And besides, he intended to say his prayers for the first time in some while, though not for himself, but for the young girls whose innocence might be torn from them before the night was through.

Sir Gotfried's Headquarters
Paris, Kingdom of France

Sir Gotfried drew the small blade across the stone, the sound of metal on rock always satisfying, always soothing. It was a daily ritual of his, to personally sharpen one of his blades. He had squires to make certain all of his swords and daggers were in prime condition and ready for battle at a moment's notice, but there was something satisfying about sharpening a blade oneself, feeling the resistance of the stone, testing the sharpness on the tip of one's finger when it was done.

And there was something particularly satisfying about the blade he now sharpened, a gift from the Grand Master himself, given to him over a decade ago, before the man had ascended to the position last year.

There was a knock at the door and his second-in-command, Sir Konrad, stepped inside. "Sir, I have news."

Gotfried continued his ritual without looking up. "What is it?"

"They know."

His chest tightened slightly. He hated incomplete statements that assumed one knew what the subject was. "Who knows what? You know how I hate it when you're cryptic like that."

Konrad shifted in position. "Sorry, sir. The Templars. They know someone has cracked their code."

Gotfried bolted upright, stabbing the tip of the dagger into the top of his desk. "Then we're too late!" He cursed, yanking the blade free then whipping it at the wall next to Konrad.

"Perhaps not."

He regarded him, the man, to his credit, not having flinched at the thrown blade. "Explain."

"Our spy said only a few know."

Gotfried paused. "Then how does *he* know?"

Konrad smiled slightly. "He's a stable boy. He's so low that no one pays attention to him, so he can go in and out without anyone caring enough to stop talking."

Gotfried joined in on the smile, taking his seat once again. "So, he overheard something?"

"Yes. Apparently, someone has arrived from Rome to investigate some fraudulent transactions."

"Who?"

"The boy didn't know the name, but he did remember the name of another knight that showed up today to meet with the investigator from Rome."

Gotfried leaned forward. "Who?"

A sneer replaced the smile. "You know him, sir. At least his name. We all do."

Gotfried growled. "Out with it!"

"Sir Marcus de Rancourt."

Gotfried's eyes widened as he fell back in his chair. Konrad was right. They *all* knew Sir Marcus de Rancourt after the events of only months ago where their kingdom had been implicated in a scandalous conspiracy. To discredit the Templars was one thing, but to also get a chance to kill Sir Marcus was another, and if he had his druthers, he'd choose the latter as the priority.

But he didn't.

He had to think of the big picture, and bringing down the Templars' financial network was his primary goal. It would further his order in the eyes of the Pope and the nobility of Europe. Yet to succeed, he had to play things very carefully, and this new bit of information, that the Templars were already aware of the fraud, was unfortunate. It meant he had to hurry, and when one did so, one was more likely to err.

He returned his attention to Konrad. "Put the word out. Find Sir Marcus. He'll lead us to this investigator from Rome."

"And when they do? Kill them?"

Gotfried frowned. "No, you fool, that will tip our hand! When you find them, let me know. I'll tell you exactly what to do to end this Templar scourge on our land once and for all."

"Very well, sir." Konrad paused. "There's one more thing."

"What?"

"The men we had watching René Courvat's house reported that some men kidnapped the younger sisters."

Gotfried's eyebrows climbed a little higher. "Interesting. They must think he's up to something. Do we know where he is yet?"

"No, he hasn't returned home since we've been watching the place."

"Odd that he'd be gone for so long, leaving them unprotected. Where did they take them?"

"To Pequin's headquarters."

Gotfried spat. "That pig of a man will have his way with them for sure."

"Should we do something?"

Gotfried frowned. "There's only one reason a man like that takes those girls."

"Sex?"

"No, leverage. He's obviously onto what René is doing, which means he probably knows where he is. I think it's time we introduced ourselves to that scum and found out what he knows."

The Shrieking Owl Tavern
Paris, Kingdom of France

"Close your eyes, Grace! No matter what you hear, keep your eyes closed!"

Grace cowered in the corner, covering her ears and squeezing her eyes shut as her sister struggled against the filthy man. She wanted to look, to see if her sister was fine, but she couldn't.

It was too terrifying a notion.

She had little understanding of these things, though she knew from what her brother had told her, and her sister in whispered conversations about boys, that some men would take what wasn't theirs to take outside of wedlock. It was called rape, and she was certain that was what was about to happen to her poor sister.

Suddenly the man cried out in pain, roaring in rage. There was a smack and her sister screamed, her outburst tearing across the room followed by a thud then silence. The door beside her flew open and she dared to allow her eyes to reveal a tiny sliver of what was going on. The bad man was kneeling on the floor, both hands gripping his private parts, and Vivienne was lying in a heap against the far wall, unmoving, blood trickling from her mouth.

"Boss, what's wrong?"

"The little bitch kicked me in the balls!"

Grace wondered why the man's private parts were called balls, but suppressed the delight in the pain he was evidently suffering.

"What do you want us to do? Kill her?"

The bad man flicked his hand toward the door. "Get them both out of here! Put them in the damned basement." He groaned. "And find me some ice!"

The man nearest her reached out and hauled her to her feet by the hair. She grabbed on, trying to ease the pain as she squealed, but it was of little use, her tiny body tossed over his shoulder as she sobbed. She twisted to see her sister carried by another man, the would-be rapist slamming the door behind them, her groaning sister's eyes fluttering for a few moments before they finally opened. Grace remained quiet, or at least as quiet as she could manage, her sobs still shaking her minute frame, though relief was slowly taking over as the horrors of only moments ago were left behind.

At least for now.

Courvat Residence
Paris, Kingdom of France

"Something definitely happened here."

Marcus agreed, Simon's observation redundant. Once Thomas had told them what he knew, he had decided it was best to find the code breaker, René Courvat, right away, despite the hour. But they were too late. A struggle had clearly occurred, a table overturned along with several chairs, and a clay bowl shattered against a wall, as if thrown in self-defense. Tanya returned from her own excursion upstairs, her calm demeanor suggesting she had found no one. "Didn't Thomas say Mr. Courvat had two younger sisters that lived with him?"

Simon headed for the stairs. "He did."

"Then I fear what may have happened to them."

"As do I." Simon headed up the stairs then returned a moment later, shaking his head. "If I had to hazard a guess, I'm thinking he's crossed the wrong person, and they've taken the young women as leverage."

Marcus frowned. "Pequin."

Simon nodded. "That's who I'm thinking. I think we should pay him a visit."

"As do I. But if we confront him, we must remember our promise to Master Thomas. No one can know it was him who told us."

Simon grunted. "I wouldn't worry about that."

Marcus regarded him. "Why?"

"Because if Pequin or any of his men have touched

those young girls, none will be alive by the end of the day to care if Thomas betrayed them."

Marcus left the drafty home and mounted his horse. He turned to his sergeant. "That's what I like about you."

Simon eyed him. "That implies there's only one thing you like, and I know you admire me for many of my fine qualities."

Marcus laughed. "You're right, of course. Besides your legendary modesty"—Simon bowed in his saddle—"it's that I always know where you'll stand on pretty much anything."

"And that is what? Kill everything in sight should I feel they've wronged some innocent in some way?"

"Exactly."

"So, you agree?"

Marcus shook his head. "No, I didn't say that. All I said is I like that I always know what you're thinking, no matter how disturbing it is."

Simon grinned. "Then I shall remain true to character so as not to disappoint." He raised a fist in the air, urging his horse forward. "Let's go kill some bad guys!"

Marcus chuckled. "One of these days, I'll get you to think before you act!" He signaled his horse after his sergeant, who shouted over his shoulder.

"And where, good sir, would be the fun in that?"

The Shrieking Owl Tavern
Paris, Kingdom of France

Pequin sat in his usual spot at the rear of the tavern, flanked by two buxom beauties who would fulfill all his desires this night, not like that little bitch earlier today. His boys were still wincing from phantom pain, the ice, stored in the cellar in a large block, providing blissful relief, then cooling his drink.

Next time I tie her down.

He took a long stare at the set of willing breasts to his left, then to his right.

Maybe tomorrow.

He downed his drink, beckoning the next fool about to enter into a contract with him at an exorbitant cost. He loved his work. What other job gave you access to all the food, drink, and women one could want, as well as the fear and respect of those around you?

All with barely lifting a finger.

At least now that he had men to do his bidding.

Someone shouted from near the entrance and everyone turned. His little piece of reserved real estate was tucked away in a corner with a wall blocking the view. He turned to his lookout, whose dropped jaw and bulging eyes suggested whatever was happening wasn't good.

"What's going on?"

The shouts were growing in number now, the din of thrown chairs and tables and the cries of pain having him rising to his own feet, his question going unanswered.

He drew his sword, sitting on the table, and swatted the ass of his lookout with it. "Answer me!"

"It's-it's knights, sir! They're killing everyone!"

He grabbed his nearest man, shoving him toward the approaching onslaught as he struggled past one of his busty delights.

She cried out in protest. "Take me with you!"

"To hell with that!" He shoved her aside, freeing himself of the corner booth, finally seeing what was happening.

And his bladder released.

He shoved his men into the fray as he tried to make it to the side exit near the bar, but it was no use. There were at least a dozen of them, in their knightly regalia, their black and white tunics worn proudly, now mostly stained in the blood of those whom he leeched off.

"There he is!" shouted one of them, and his heart fluttered as he realized the knight was pointing at him. The massacre continued, men and women gored, sliced open, no mercy shown.

For they were after only one man.

And that man was him.

Why?

What had he ever done to them? He was extremely careful to never do anything that might raise the hackles of any of the religious orders—it was simply too dangerous, and they were too powerful. His men weren't even fighting back, all now hiding under tables or struggling toward the one other door known only to the regulars.

Unfortunately, almost everyone here was a regular,

and the door was blocked, no one able to open it as it swung inward, and half a dozen people were pressed against it by those behind them.

He wasn't getting out that way.

Second floor.

He turned for the stairs when something hit him in the shoulder. He winced, grabbing for the source of the pain, finding nothing beyond something wet and warm. He stared at his hand and his knees buckled at the sight of the bright crimson blood now soaking his fingers. He turned back to find one of the knights on his heels, his sword, slick with blood, swinging at him.

Pequin dropped to his knees, partially to avoid the blow, partially because he had lost all strength, fear overwhelming him.

The blade sliced over his head, missing it by a finger if that, and he sucked in a quick breath, pushing forward on his hands and knees, when a powerful force gripped the back of his shirt, lifting him off the ground, then tossing him back into his booth, the table shattering underneath him.

He struggled to turn, to face what was to come, the knight rounding the corner, his sword extended in front of him, the tip aimed directly at Pequin's throat.

"You are Hamon Pequin?"

"Y-yes."

The wails and screams of terror continued out of sight, the remaining attackers determined to finish what they had started.

"Where is the code breaker?"

Pequin's eyes widened. "The code breaker? Wh-what do you mean?"

The blade inched closer. "You know what I mean. Answer me, or die most horribly."

"Do you mean René?"

"Yes. René Courvat."

Pequin's eyes bulged at the revelation they weren't here for him. "Yes. He's the one you want. Not me! Spare me, and I'll tell you everything."

The man took another step closer, the tip of the blade now pressed against Pequin's neck. "You'll tell me everything I want to know, then *I'll* decide whether I let you live."

Pequin didn't like the terms of the deal, yet he had no choice. "I can tell you where he lives, it's not far, but he's n-not there."

The man frowned. "Where is he?"

"I-I don't know."

The blade pressed against his neck and a trickle of blood ran down toward his chest as he tilted his head back as far as he could, pressing into the bench behind him.

"I swear, I don't know." His eyes shot wide. "But I've got a man following him! I can take you to him!"

Four knights rushed past, their footfalls heading upstairs and downstairs suggesting they intended to be thorough in their depravity. And he knew he was going to die. The only question now was how painful it would be.

And when.

"Yes, I can take you to him."

"Where is he?"

"I-I don't know exactly. Outside of Paris."

"Then how is that of any use to us?"

"I-I can find him. I swear!"

"I don't believe you." The sword pressed against his neck again.

Alain!

"Wait!"

The man stopped.

"Alain! Find Alain! He'll take you to him."

"Where's he?"

"At his home, just go out the door then right, follow the road for a short bit. It's a black and white rooming house with a big cross painted on the door. You can't miss it."

One of the knights appeared, drenched in blood. "We're done, sir."

"Excellent work. Tell the men we've got one more job to do."

The knights from earlier reappeared, two of them carrying René's sisters over their shoulders, the young girls crying and wailing.

"Hey, where are you taking them?"

The man, obviously in charge, regarded him. "Why should you care?"

"They're mine."

"That doesn't match my information."

Pequin watched as the girls disappeared around the corner, the sound of the bar emptying out providing him with a hint of hope he might yet survive. "Please, let me live, and I won't tell anyone what happened here!"

"I'm afraid that's not possible."

Pequin's eyes bulged. "But we had a deal!"

"Did we?"

His shoulders slumped. "I thought you Hospitallers were supposed to be men of honor!"

The man took one step back, withdrawing his sword. He eyed him for a moment, a smile creeping on his face. "Now, *that's* an interesting notion, that."

Pequin's eyes narrowed. "Huh?"

The man's smile spread as he wagged a finger. "Sorry, but if I told you, then your wonderful idea might go to waste."

He stepped forward, thrusting his sword into Pequin's stomach before twisting it then yanking it free. Pequin grabbed at the ever-increasing rush of blood staining his shirt, the pain rapidly overwhelming him as he stared up at the knight, sworn, he had thought, to serve the Church.

Not slaughter the people they purported to protect.

The man sheathed his sword. "Enjoy the rest of your evening."

The Shrieking Owl Tavern
Paris, Kingdom of France

"Something's wrong."

Marcus sniffed the air as his sergeant had just done, prompted by a growl from Tanya. He recognized the smell immediately. Death. Blood had been spilled here recently. A lot of it. The stench of disembowelment and the foul odor of released bowels in the moment of death filled the air. He dismounted, tying his horse up and drawing his sword. "Be careful."

Simon drew his own sword and they approached the entrance of the tavern that, according to Thomas, apparently served as the base of operations for Pequin, the man manipulating René into doing his bidding, and perhaps the kidnapper of two young innocents. Simon cautiously pushed open the door and Marcus' eyes widened at the disturbing sight that lay before them.

Bodies were strewn about everywhere. Tables and chairs were tipped over, the floor swam in blood, and the walls were sprayed with the aftermath of what could only have been caused by swords slicing through human flesh.

It reminded him of a battlefield in the Holy Land, though few of these people were armed, and those that were wore no armor or protective gear, likely Pequin's henchmen.

"Whoever did this knew what they were doing."

Marcus agreed. "They either took their dead with them, or suffered no casualties."

There was a groan from the back and Tanya bared her teeth, growling.

"Stay," ordered Marcus as they advanced toward the sound. Rounding a corner, they found a man sitting on the floor, gored through the stomach, his face pale, his chest heaving rapidly as he took his last breaths.

Marcus kneeled beside him as Simon kept watch. "What's your name?"

"Hamon Pequin."

How fortunate.

"Who did this?"

"H-Hospitallers."

"Bullshit."

Marcus agreed with his sergeant's assessment. "I find that impossible to believe."

"I-it's true. They just left."

"How do you—"

"Their tunics. Black and white, with a cross. It was them, I swear."

"But why?"

"It was that bastard René. They were looking for him."

Marcus' eyebrows shot up. "Because he broke the code?"

If Pequin could pale any further, he did. "Y-you know?"

"Yes."

Pequin's shoulders slumped. "Then what was the point of all this if you already know?"

"They don't know we know." Marcus glanced about. "Where are René's sisters?"

"Th-they took them."

Another thing that didn't sound like Hospitallers. "Why?"

"How the hell should I know?"

Tanya, rounding the corner, her last command ignored, growled, and Pequin recoiled.

"Keep him away from me."

Marcus glanced at the mastiff and she sat, panting. "*He* is a *she*, and more of a lady than the likes you have ever known." Tanya rubbed her nose against Marcus' hand, as if she knew she had been paid a compliment.

Simon glared at the man. "They obviously plan to use them as leverage, just like this scum wanted to."

Marcus agreed. "We have to find René before they do." He stared down at the dying man. "Do you know where he is?"

"Why should I tell you?"

"Because in the next few moments, you'll be meeting Saint Peter, and should you help us, we might be able to save those girls, and bring those who did this to justice."

Pequin glared at him for a moment, then sighed. "Fine. I don't know, but Lyon does."

"Where can we find him?"

"S-south of the city." Pequin was growing weak, and Marcus sensed these might be his last words. "Find Alain, he'll tell you."

"And where can we find him?"

"Out the door, to the right. There's a house, about a mile from here, painted like those damned Hospitallers…"

Pequin gasped, his eyes bulging, and his entire body shook. Marcus reached out and held the man's shoulder, staring into his eyes, providing the dying man some comfort in his final moments.

Then he was still.

Marcus made the sign of the cross, saying a silent prayer for the deeply flawed man, leaving his final judgment in God's hands. He rose and turned to Simon. "Let's get out of here. We need to find this Alain he spoke of before the Hospitallers do."

Simon shook his head as they made for the entrance. "I still can't believe they're behind this."

"Neither can I, yet he described their tunics, and this"—he waved his hand at the gruesome scene—"was done by skilled warriors."

"We should warn the fortress."

Marcus nodded. "You're right. If the Hospitallers know the code has been broken, then the damage may already be irreversible."

Alain's Residence
Paris, Kingdom of France

Alain bolted upright in bed, glancing about the darkened room, wondering what had awoken him. Heavy footfalls on the outside stairs that clung to the building, giving access to the second floor, was his terrifying answer.

That many men, in that much of a hurry, couldn't be good, and only six people had rooms up here, so the odds were uncomfortably close for him being the target, especially considering his profession.

He rolled out of bed, stuffing his feet into his boots, the rest of his clothes still on to save him precious moments in the morning. He tiptoed to the window, peering through the cracks, only to have his heart racing at the sight.

Half a dozen mounted men, all holding someone else's horse, were milling about below, all wearing the armor of knights.

If they were here for him, it couldn't be for any good reason, and with Pequin now involved in stealing from the Templars, anything was possible when it came to religious orders.

He had to get out of here.

Yet the lone exit besides the window was the door.

Somebody pounded on it but he paid it no mind, his window already thrown open. He climbed out, a narrow stretch of thatch the only thing between him and the ground below where either a broken neck or whatever fate these new arrivals had in store for him awaited. He skirted the side of the building, and for a moment he thought he might get away with it, when he heard his door give way to the pounding, and a head shoved out the window behind him.

"Stop!"

Six heads turned.

Six swords unsheathed.

He cursed, clearing the corner as he heard the whinny of horses as the knights below began their pursuit.

He had precious moments. He sprinted the few paces he had left then jumped, clearing the narrow alleyway between his boarding house and the baker next door, landing on the roof, his shoe piercing the tightly bound straw. He struggled to free it, finally succeeding, only to find his foot bare.

And the pounding of hoofs nearing, as well as the shouts of those pursuing him from the roof next door.

He scrambled over the peak of the roof and slid down the opposite side, leaping to the next, this time the roof thankfully holding, and he continued his awkward sprint, all the while heading slightly to the right and away from the street those on horseback now occupied.

He spotted the Swan Tavern, a stack of empty barrels behind it, and smiled. He slid to the ground, rushed across the street, and popped the top off one of the barrels, climbing inside. He carefully slid the lid back in place as the horses pounded by, the shouts from overhead fading as his pursuers desperately sought him.

Then there was silence.

And a smile.

Something squeaked then brushed past his ankle. He shuddered and punched the lid clear as he erupted from the barrel, already occupied by the infestation that gripped every modern city.

A throat cleared behind him and he spun to find a lone knight, his black and white tunic stained with blood, his sword unsheathing.

Alain belted him in the face, knocking him out cold.

He then stole his boots and sprinted for safety.

A safety he was sadly mistaken about.

For as he rushed inside the Shrieking Owl Tavern, he was overwhelmed with the carnage inside, nothing moving, nothing having escaped unscathed, the blood on the knight's tunic explained.

They had killed them all.

And it had to be because of the Templars' code.

That meant they must have been looking for René.

I have to find him.

And that meant he had to find Lyon.

But he'd need a horse first.

Sir Gotfried's Headquarters
Paris, Kingdom of France

"The mission was a success."

Gotfried eyed his second, Konrad, then took an exaggerated look at the empty space behind the man. "I don't see our code breaker."

Konrad flushed though quickly recovered. "What I meant was we successfully conducted the raid, recovered René Courvat's sisters, interrogated Pequin himself, and made sure no witnesses were left."

"Yet I still see no code breaker."

"No, but we have an excellent lead."

Gotfried leaned back. "And that is?"

"Pequin confirmed that René is currently outside of the city, and is being followed by one of his men. This can only mean that he is redeeming fraudulent Letters of Credit, and will return shortly. I've left two men to watch his house, and they'll grab him when he returns for his sisters." Konrad raised his chin slightly. "It's only a matter of time before we have him in our custody."

Gotfried regarded his second for a moment. It wasn't the outcome he had wanted, yet it was the best they could hope for under the circumstances. There was no chance René would abandon his sisters, from what he had been told of the man, and if he were redeeming his clever forgeries, it was a reasonable explanation as to why he wasn't at home.

And Konrad was right. The man would return

shortly, and they would take him.

A successful mission, if not timely.

Though he wasn't done with his second.

"Very well." He waved a finger. "In your zeal to kill everyone, did you happen to interrogate any of them before spilling their blood?"

Konrad flushed, his tunic still stained from the evening's events. "I…yes, I did, though only a few. Most were bar patrons who would know little regardless, and the others who might, tried to engage us for the most part."

"No doubt dying to protect their leader, Pequin?"

Konrad nodded, a little too eagerly at the plausible explanation. "Yes, no doubt."

It was bullshit. He knew men like Pequin and the type that served him. Loyalty lasted while the power was in place. Once that power was threatened, once someone more powerful came along, allegiances switched, tongues loosened, and swords dropped.

And the moment his knights entered the tavern, Pequin was no longer the alpha male.

He was but a lamb.

Those that died weren't trying to save him, they were trying to save themselves.

And if disarmed, or forced to surrender, they would have spilled everything with the slightest of provocations.

Though if René was indeed outside the city, doing what he always did, with a tail on him assigned by Pequin, then Pequin obviously wasn't concerned that his source of untold wealth was at risk of running, nor should he be.

One of his men rushed into the room, bowing deeply. "I'm sorry to interrupt, sirs, but Pequin's man, Alain, eluded capture."

Gotfried pursed his lips, the name unfamiliar, and curiously absent from Konrad's report. "Alain?"

Konrad flushed slightly. "Sorry, sir, I neglected to mention that Pequin gave us the name of one of his men who was to rendezvous with René's tail south of the city today."

Gotfried regarded him for a moment, his second shifting uncomfortably in place. "An important piece of information to neglect to mention, don't you think?"

Konrad bowed slightly. "Yes, sir, of course."

Gotfried turned to the new arrival. "And this Alain eluded you?"

"Yes, sir. He must have heard us coming. He escaped out a window and across several rooftops." The man rubbed his jaw. "I almost had him, but…"

Gotfried leaned to the side slightly, getting a better view of the bruised chin. "He packs quite the wallop, that one."

The man grunted. "He does, that."

Gotfried returned his focus to Konrad. "Who gave the order to capture him?"

Konrad squared his shoulders. "I did."

"And you didn't think it might have been a better idea to simply follow him, and have him lead us directly to René?"

Konrad's mouth opened slightly, confusion on his face. "I-I…"

Gotfried dismissed the uncharacteristic stammering. "What do you suggest we do now that your plan has failed?"

Konrad recovered, his jaw snapping shut. "We wait for him to return home." He turned to the new arrival. "You did leave two men to watch the tavern as I instructed?"

"Yes, sir."

Gotfried leaned back. "Good. Then I have little doubt they are now following this Alain, and will report back to us shortly, perhaps even with René in custody."

Konrad appeared puzzled. "Sir? I don't understand."

Gotfried frowned, slowly shaking his head at his second's lack of foresight. "Let me ask you this. If you were Alain, and a bunch of men just tried to capture or kill you, and you had no idea what had just happened to Pequin and his men, what would you do?"

Konrad smiled slightly. "I'd go back to the tavern and tell my boss what had just happened."

"Exactly, and when he finds them all dead, where do you think he'll go?"

Konrad shook his head at his own stupidity, his smile spreading. "To meet up with his partner, south of the city."

"Exactly." He gestured at Konrad's blood-soaked tunic. "Now, get yourself cleaned up."

Konrad bowed. "Yes, sir, but there's one more thing I'd like to discuss with you. An…idea, if you will."

"What is it?"

"A way we might leverage this situation, with no risk to ourselves."

Gotfried dismissed the other knight with a flick of his wrist, then folded his arms as he leaned back. "Tell me.”

Arcueil, Kingdom of France

René rose and stretched, the inn he had stayed at a reasonable one, his room a treat to himself with the extra funds he had. It had been a foolish, selfish indulgence, realized as soon as he had closed the door the night before.

He sighed.

Money unearned has no value.

He now understood the nobility a little better. They were born into their money, therefore had no need to earn it. It explained the lavish lifestyles and ridiculous indulgences. He could have slept in the stable with his horse, in fact, he could have slept outside of town on the ground, yet instead, he had paid for a room with money meant to secure his sisters' futures.

He gripped the heavy purse in his hand, swearing to never waste a single coin again.

He peered out the window, the sun already too high in the sky. Another price extracted from him by his indulgence of the night before. Now he would have to ride even harder if he expected to keep on schedule, for he feared his description might already have been sent to Paris, where no doubt someone far cleverer than him was at work determining who it was defrauding them.

Though that wasn't his biggest concern.

It was his sisters, for they were alone, with no one to watch out for them, and the men involved were not the type to be trusted. His heart hammered as he thought of their poor innocent souls, and what might happen should Pequin discover what he was up to.

He marched for the door, determined to move all the more faster, and perhaps complete the loop ahead of schedule.

Please, Lord, watch over them for me while I'm gone, then I'll take care of the rest.

Templar Barracks
Vincennes, Kingdom of France

Damase shoveled in the last spoonful of breakfast, pushing the bowl away. A stout porridge was always welcome, especially on what he was certain would prove a brisk morning, an unusual frost having rolled in overnight. He would head back to the fortress, stopping at a couple of outposts along the way, though bypassing most of the loop the thieves had been using.

There was no point in visiting any of them beyond reconfirming his theory that a single, unique individual would complete a circuit each week. All the data he needed would be arriving at the fortress over the coming days, and if his theory held, he'd apprehend the latest culprit within the next few days, and that person would hopefully lead him to the ringleader.

He left the comforts of the outpost then mounted his horse, heading west, toward Paris, his pace leisurely until he left the town. He was about to urge his mount to go faster when he heard the distinct snap of a crossbow behind him. He ducked down and to the side, the bolt whipping past him, missing by inches. Rather than run, he tugged the reins to the left, turning his beast around as he drew his sword, and as he suspected, he found himself facing off against the two Hospitallers from the day before.

Both drew their swords, the crossbow tossed aside by the man-child.

"Do you two really want to engage a Templar Knight in battle?"

"You're an old man," said the second. "You'll rue the day when you mocked my friend, then didn't have the courage to meet his challenge."

"Is that what it was? I didn't have a dog with me to tell me what he was saying, your friend's voice so high."

"You bastard!"

It was laughable, if it weren't backed up by rage-filled eyes, the need for vengeance clear.

Yet he didn't have time for this.

"Look, I apologize for my disrespect yesterday, I meant no harm by it, and it was merely in response to taunts from both of you. Let us shake hands as men of honor, and go our separate ways."

The man-child held his sword high. "We'll go our separate ways when I separate your head from your neck, Templar!"

The two charged, the squealer in the lead, his sword held too high, his inexperience obvious. Damase signaled his well-trained horse forward, and the beast snorted, eager for the excitement as he carried his master into battle. Damase, his sword pointed forward at chest level, prepared for the first battle he had been in for some time, his shoulder aching with the effort. If his opponents survived more than two or three blows, this battle could be lost.

And he had more important things to do besides die on the outskirts of some unimportant town, all because an insecure man couldn't take an insult.

The man-child's sword dropped, his opponent no doubt hoping to cleave him in the chest.

A foolish move.

Damase adjusted his sword slightly to the left, catching his opponent's and redirecting it to the right, along with his own blade, which, as they passed each other, was now perpendicular to the man-child.

And at neck height.

Damase's shoulder roared in agony as he struggled to hold it in place, the sudden relief a moment later indicating victory. He turned quickly to see the man's head bounce off the back of his horse then roll onto the ground, his friend crying out in horror. Damase turned to face him.

"Leave now, and you shall live. Stay, and you will meet the same fate as your friend."

The Hospitaller stared at him for a moment, his chest heaving, then tossed his sword, smacking his horse and sending them both charging back into town, where he might have friends.

Damase said a silent prayer for his opponent's foolish soul, then urged his horse forward toward Paris again, unwilling to perhaps face greater numbers, and still with no time to waste. He would report the incident at the next outpost, and keep a wary eye on any further Hospitallers he might encounter.

They are clearly emboldened by something.

And he was certain what it was. King Philip had likely indicated his support in some way, and they felt the Templars' days were numbered in the Kingdom of France.

He frowned, for they might be right, should he not bring the code breakers to justice.

Thibault Residence
Paris, Kingdom of France

"What is it? What have you done?"

Thomas shrank in his chair, avoiding eye contact with Simone. "Umm, nothing?"

She rolled her eyes. "My God, you're the worst liar I have ever met, young man. Do you realize I know every single time you are lying to me? Fortunately for you, you rarely do it about anything important, so I let it slide." She jabbed a finger at him. "But not today! Too much is at stake right now, and I can't afford any slip ups." She leaned closer to him. "What is it that you're not telling me?"

"Nothing." He glanced up at her briefly, his eyes darting away from her unconvinced glare. "I, umm, I'm, well, depressed."

She stood straight and he risked another glance. Her voice softened. "Depressed? Whatever for? You have money, a roof, food." She snapped her fingers as a smile emerged. "It's a woman, isn't it? You need a little fun in your life." She lowered her voice. "I'll send one of the girls over after work. Enjoy yourself. You've earned it."

He shook his head in horror. "Oh, no, please don't."

She grinned. "Fine. I'll send two!" He gasped and her eyes narrowed. "Or do you prefer boys? I can arrange that as well." Her grin revealed teeth. "Or both?"

He waved his hands in front of him, his eyes

squeezed shut as he futilely blocked the images created by his inexperienced mind. "Oh, God, no, please. I just want to be left alone."

She stopped, her foot now tapping, and he opened his eyes, the images playing out on the back of his eyelids terrifying. She was frowning down at him. "Well, you're alone now, and you don't look happy. Whatever happened to that lass you were doting on, the one who lives in Crécy-la-Chapelle near Sir Marcus? I thought you were sweet on her?"

He shrugged. "It's complicated."

She grunted. "Well, love always is." She leaned forward, pressing a finger on his desk, the knuckle going white. "Don't keep things from me. I always know. Life changing things are afoot, and I can't have lovelorn romantics screwing things up because they can't keep their mouth shut."

He flushed at the memory of the verbal diarrhea that had revealed all at Marcus' prompting. "Yes, ma'am."

"Good." She straightened. "Anything else to tell me?"

He shook his head.

"Then get to work. I've got an important meeting in an hour." She hurried away and Thomas breathed a sigh of relief. If he had mentioned a word about Marcus having stayed at his home, she would have known immediately that he had spilled his guts, telling them everything. Though the very act had terrified him, for something more was going on than he had been told, it had been such a relief to tell two of the few friends he had in this world, and perhaps the only two men who might be able to do something about it. Though what that might be, he wasn't sure.

And none of it solved his ultimate problem. What to do about sweet Isabelle?

Templar Outpost
St. Mandel, Kingdom of France

Damase opened the door to the outpost and stepped aside as a civilian, startled, excused himself. He dismissed the apology with a wave of his hand, then noticed the man appeared nervous.

"Are you ill?"

The man flinched at the question, adding further evidence to Damase's suspicions. "Umm, yes. Just a bit of a, umm, stomach bug, I'm afraid. I-I'll be fine."

Damase pursed his lips in sympathy. "Those can be nasty."

"I blame my wife's cooking."

Damase laughed. "I feel your pain. The Order has been trying to poison me for years, but I haven't yet been able to prove it." He bowed slightly. "Enjoy your day, good sir."

The man nodded. "You too, sir." He hurried across the street, toward a tied up horse, and Damase entered the Templar outpost, hailing the knight manning the front desk and quickly confirming that the last two loops he had detected were executed by men matching the same descriptions as before.

He had found the pattern, and it didn't help him.

He wrote out a quick report on the incident with the Hospitallers, handing the paper to his counterpart.

"I'll file this at once. Are you injured?"

Damase shrugged, wincing at his overtasked shoulder. "I escaped relatively unscathed, though my old wound is now demanding attention. I can't say the same for my opponents. I dispatched one and allowed the other to surrender without dignity."

"Too bad you didn't remove them both from existence. These Hospitallers are getting continually worse. They have no honor. No dignity. The entire order should be disbanded."

Damase grunted. "I concur." He changed the subject back to his true purpose as his report was folded and sealed, then handed off to a messenger. "Did you get the new directives yet?"

"Which ones? The ones that say I must immediately send descriptions to the fortress of every man who comes in here redeeming a Letter of Credit? The one that means I have barely enough horses or messengers for the regular business I'm expected to conduct here?" He growled. "Whatever imbecile ordered that, should be drawn and quartered."

Damase bristled, though decided it best not to take credit. "I'm sure most would agree." He rose. "I'll bother you no further, as you are obviously busy." He stepped outside, drawing a deep breath as he calmed himself, and cursed his aching shoulder. He understood the man's frustrations, and would share them if he didn't know their purpose.

Yet he did.

And if the man inside was aware of the gravity of the situation, he would never dare question the wisdom of the orders.

René mounted his horse and quickly headed north, his entire body shaking from his encounter moments ago. He had to keep it together. His constant nerves were getting the better of him, and his doubts as to whether anyone had noticed were torn asunder by an innocent question from a concerned Templar.

Are you ill?

An innocuous question on a normal day, but not today, not when he was stealing from an incredibly powerful organization answerable only to the Pope himself.

He smiled slightly.

The stomach bug excuse had played well, and he was impressed he had come up with it so quickly.

Remember that for any future encounters.

But should there be any future encounters? He was almost done with his loop, and had more money than he had ever known filling his saddlebags. If he aborted his mission and simply returned home now, then he could collect his sisters and head north. He might not have enough money should the worst case scenario of being unable to find employment at their new home play out, but if he did, then there was already more than enough.

Yet he was so close to being done, so close to having enough for any possible outcome, that he was torn between what was prudent, and what was possible. He closed his eyes, sighing, as he left the small town behind.

Lord, what should I do? What would you *do?*

He frowned. He certainly wouldn't be stealing from those sworn to serve Him. He opened his eyes, staring at the road ahead. A turn to the left, and he was headed home. It was a simple choice, an obvious choice.

You know what to say now.

He squared his shoulders.

A stomach bug.

It was so simple, so common, that anyone would believe it. And the little bit about his wife's cooking was something any man could appreciate.

Though perhaps not a Templar, as they were sworn to celibacy.

I wonder what that must be like.

He grunted.

Not much different than your own life, you fool!

He stared at the road back to Paris he had passed, surprised at himself, though pleased. If only he could show this much courage and determination when it came to women, then perhaps he'd have a wife by now, children even.

It would be nice to have a family.

His sisters were almost like his children, since he had been forced to raise them, especially little Grace, but eventually they would be gone. They didn't suffer his afflictions, and would make wonderful wives one day.

Then he'd be alone.

All alone.

His chest ached at the prospect.

I want someone to share my life with.

His eyes burned with the loneliness he now felt, the overwhelming wave of pity consuming him.

The whinny of a horse behind him caused him to snap out of his reverie. He glanced over his shoulder and tensed, the man, some distance back, appearing familiar.

Am I being followed?

Alain's Residence
Paris, Kingdom of France

Marcus stared at the two-story house in front of them, it, like most of the other structures in the area, having seen much better days. "Could this be it?"

Simon shrugged. "It must be. It's the only thing remotely close to Pequin's description. At least it's the same colors." He pointed at the faded paint on the door. "And I guess that was a cross at some point."

Marcus spotted some people talking nearby, anxiously glancing at the building and the Templars. He guided his horse toward them. After fruitlessly searching for Alain's rooming house in the dark, they had returned to the fortress and spent the night rather than disturb Thomas again. A full report had been provided to Sir Matthew in the morning, and now, with the city awake, they hoped to find the man Pequin had referred to, Alain.

He nodded at the crowd. "Good day to you. Can you tell me if a man named Alain lives here?"

Hushed whispers were exchanged, one of the men finally replying. "Are you after him too?"

Marcus' eyes narrowed, his question answered, though curiously. "What do you mean?"

"He was chased out of here by men with swords last night. It was quite the racket, I tell you. Serves him right, though. He's a scoundrel, that one, hanging with Pequin's crowd. He used to be such a well-mannered boy, though always a bit odd. Simple, you know."

"Probably kicked in the head by a goat when he was younger," cackled a toothless woman, eliciting some laughter from her companions.

The man agreed. "Coulda been, coulda been. Nobody ever paid him any respect because of it. Maybe that's why he joined those criminals."

"Shush!" hissed the woman. "Someone might hear you!"

He dismissed her admonishment. "I don't care. I don't owe him any money."

"No need to worry," reassured Marcus. "We're aware of what he was."

"He was a brutal one. You never wanted to be late with him." He paused as he picked up on what was just said. "Was? So, it's true then, he's dead?"

Marcus nodded. "He is."

"Are you sure?"

"Yes, I saw it with my own eyes. He as well as everyone he was with is dead."

Smiles and hugs abounded as the tragic loss of life was celebrated, the man finally turning his attention back to the Templars on horseback. "This is good news. I would like to thank whoever it is that killed him, for they have done us a great service."

Marcus ignored the distasteful though understandable thoughts. "So, you don't know who did this?"

The man shook his head. "No."

Marcus frowned. "The men who were here looking for Alain, did they have surcoats or tunics that identified them?"

"You mean were they Templars?"

Snickers abounded and Marcus smiled. "No, I'm sure they weren't from our order, but perhaps they were from some other."

The man shook his head. "I heard them and looked out the window, but it was too dark. Their tunics might have been black, but then again, they could have been purple or white for all I could tell."

That's unfortunate.

"And you say Alain got away?"

"Aye, he did. I saw him running across the rooftops. A quick one that boy always was."

"But not with the brain!" cried the woman, the gathering crowd erupting in laughter.

Marcus smiled slightly, feeling sorry for what must have been a difficult childhood. "Any idea where he might go if he were in trouble?"

The man shrugged, then his eyes widened. "His father! He lives not far from here, though I'm not sure if they really speak. He was none too pleased with the crowd his son took up with, I hear."

"Could you show us?"

The man eyed him. "What's in it for me?"

Marcus smiled. "I'll put in a good word with the Lord for you."

"I'd prefer gold." He gave the others a look. "Or perhaps one of those famous Letters of Credit. They seem to be getting handed out quite a bit lately."

Marcus tensed. "What do you mean?"

Glances that were too knowing were exchanged among those gathered, one of the women quickly turning and rushing away when he made eye contact.

"I mean, if you have money to throw around, then

throw some of it my way, and I'll take you to his father's place. If you don't, then find him yourself."

Marcus watched the departing woman out of the corner of his eye. "I'm afraid we're forbidden from carrying more than four deniers on our person."

The man batted a hand at him. "Then forget it." He turned away, the others following, and Marcus realized there was no use in pursuing the conversation.

But all was not lost.

He urged his horse after the woman, finding her on the next street.

"Ma'am, may I trouble you for a moment?"

She glanced up at him, continuing to quickly shuffle away. "Why? I've done nothing wrong! Please, leave me alone!"

Her reaction was curious, and if anything, made him even more suspicious than a moment ago. "I never said you did, ma'am. I merely require a moment of your time."

She came to an abrupt halt, staring up at him, her hands on her hips in defiance, her bravado false, if her trembling lip was any indication. "What? What is it then?"

"Do you know the man named Alain we were speaking of?"

"I know of him, but we are not acquainted, if that's what you mean."

"Do you know where we might find his father?"

"No."

Her reply was a little too quick, delivered before he had a chance to finish his question, her eyes, darting away, the final giveaway. "I think you do."

She paled. "I don't, I swear, but…"

He had her.

"But what?"

"Well, umm, my husband knows."

"And where might we find him?"

"Why are you looking for Alain? Is it because of what René has been doing?"

Marcus regarded her, deciding not to tip his hand. "And what has René been doing?"

She frowned. "Well, if you don't know, then I'm not telling you."

"What if I told you that Alain and his friends kidnapped René's sisters, and we're trying to find them?"

Her eyes bulged. "Why? So you can use them against him?"

"Of course not. We're monks, not criminals. We hope to save them from whoever has them, then find René to discuss, shall we say, matters of great importance."

She took a step forward. "He's a good man. He's only trying to help people like us."

"Like us?"

She stepped back. "I've said too much."

"Perhaps not. Perhaps if you tell us the *entire* truth, we might be more lenient on a man who is only trying to help."

She stared up at him. "What do you mean?"

"Well, at the moment, as far as the Order is concerned, René is a thief and a fraudster, and what he has done merits death."

She gasped. "No!"

He held up a finger. "Perhaps, however, if we knew more, I might be able to save him, but I can only do that if you loosen your tongue, and share what you know."

She hesitated, scratching at her shoulder with the opposite hand. "I, umm, think you should speak with my husband."

Marcus dismounted. "Please, lead the way."

Templar Outpost
St. Mandel, Kingdom of France

Damase inspected his horse, and was about to mount when a messenger stepped out of the outpost, flagging him down.

"Excuse me, sir, but are you Sir Damase de Sissey?"

"I am."

The messenger smiled, opening his bag. "I have dispatches here meant for you from several outposts. I'm to deliver them to you at the fortress, but inside they said you were here. Do you want them now, or should I leave them in Paris for you?"

Damase shook his head. "No, I'll take them now."

The young man handed over half a dozen folded pages, noting the delivery on his manifest before rushing off to deliver his remaining messages. Damase returned to the outpost, acknowledging the others inside, then took a seat, breaking the seal on the first message. He quickly scanned the contents, the descriptions of the transactions as detailed as he could have hoped for, then opened the second message. He began the third then paused.

He reread the description, then flipped through the others, finding similar descriptions, all from transactions within the past day, all in the counterclockwise loop around the city.

Could it be?

He opened the next dispatch and his mouth widened as he found another matching transaction.

Located here, only moments ago.

He leaped to his feet, rushing toward the knight still manning his post. He tossed the dispatch on the table, jabbing his finger on it. "This man that was just here. Describe him!"

The man glanced at the page then tapped the description. "I did. Right here." He jutted his chin toward the door. "You walked right past him when you came in."

Damase squinted as he struggled to remember, his mind not what it once was when it came to irrelevant interactions. He gasped as the memory was found. "You mean the one with the stomach bug?"

"I don't know about that, but come to think of it, he didn't appear well."

"Have you ever seen him before?"

He shrugged. "I don't think so, but I can't be sure. I see a lot of people." He thought for a moment, scratching his beard. "You know, maybe I have. I think a couple of times, maybe?"

Damase struggled to contain his excitement. "And the amounts. Were they small or large?"

"I'm not sure about before, but today's was large, at least for his type."

"What do you mean?"

The man shrugged. "Well, he's obviously not nobility, now, is he?"

Damase had to agree. And he had to act. "Send a dispatch to Paris that I think this is the man I've been looking for."

"Why him? What's he done?"

Damase ignored the questions, rushing out the

door, peering in all directions for the man, but coming up empty. He leaped on his horse and headed north, the direction the man had been going when he last saw him, though for all he knew he might have doubled back to the south.

He had to take a chance and commit.

North it is.

He said a silent prayer, then urged his steed forward, and hopefully toward the answers he was so desperately in search of.

Thibault Residence
Paris, Kingdom of France

Simone sat in her office, staring into nothingness, her mind racing with the myriad of possibilities of how what she had gotten herself into could go wrong. Gotfried was not to be trusted. She pursed her lips. That wasn't entirely accurate. He was a knight, after all. He could be trusted to keep his word. It was his word that should be feared.

For it could mean death.

The beating laid upon her husband had certainly aided the smallpox that ultimately took him. They had shown him no quarter when he had begged for extra time, for relief from the crushing payments.

And Gotfried had been true to his word.

He had exacted a toll from her poor, dear husband.

As promised when the loan was initially negotiated.

Oh, how I miss you, my love.

Her chest ached and her eyes burned as she closed them, picturing the man she loved in his final days, the sight disturbing to say the least. His body was covered with the infection, the pustules terrifying to behold, yet she had forced a smile in his dying days, keeping his hands wrapped and his body covered, so he never had to see the horror that had stricken him.

And he had been so brave. He knew he was dying, yet his only concern had been her, and how he had never given her children.

She gasped, and turned her chair to face the corner,

lest anyone enter and catch her in this moment of weakness. For Simone Thibault could never show she had a heart, could never show she was human like those that owed her, that she cried almost every day with the loss of her beloved, and the empty home he had left her with.

She had wanted children. She always had. Yet for some reason, she could never get pregnant. Whether it was her fault or his, she didn't know.

And it didn't matter.

She would never be with another man, for she had found and lost her one true love.

Her poor, foolish love, who had left her with such a crippling debt, she was barely getting by despite her success, and the airs she put on. If what she had started worked, and Gotfried and his minions forgave her the debt left her by her husband, she could put the negatives of that chapter of her life behind her, and instead enjoy only the good times, never again blaming her husband for his inept business decisions.

She would be free.

They would be free.

But only if it worked.

And so much could go wrong.

She blasted a breath through her pursed lips, her shoulders sagging as she attempted to ease the tension dominating her.

And failed.

There was simply too much that could go wrong, and if Gotfried blamed her, it would be the end of everything.

And everyone.

She sighed, turning her chair back to face the doorway, the sound of Thomas working away in his room causing her growing concern.

And she made a decision.

"Thomas!"

His chair scraped the floor then he emerged, rushing down the hall and into her office.

"Yes, ma'am?"

"I want you to take a few days off."

Thomas' eyebrows rose. "Really? But there's so much work to do."

"That's not important, at least not right now. I want you to take a few days off, and wait to hear from me or Enzo before you come back."

His eyes narrowed. "Why?"

She regarded him for a moment, wondering how much she should tell him. He already knew too much, though he knew nothing of Gotfried and the order the man commanded in this wretched city. Yet that little bit of knowledge, the fact he knew the Templar code had been broken, and by whom, could be enough to get the poor boy killed should things go wrong and Gotfried seek vengeance. "Something is happening, and it could be dangerous."

"What?"

"I can't say."

"Does it have to do with René?"

Bloody hell, boy, stop being so smart!

"What makes you think that?"

He shrugged. "It's the only thing of interest that's happened around here in a while."

She shook her head. "Sometimes, you're too smart

for your own good." She leaned forward. "I want you out of here. In fact, why don't you go visit that girl you're always pining over. If you leave now, you can be there before nightfall. I'll send for you when it's safe."

Thomas paled slightly. "Is it really that dangerous?"

She frowned then sighed. "I'm afraid, my boy, in my haste, I may have made a mistake that could cost us all dearly."

He stood in front of her, saying nothing, his eyes taking on the look she knew meant he was thinking hard, attempting to solve the problem of the day. His eyes widened. "What about Sir Marcus? Perhaps he can help."

She laughed. "If he only knew, he'd kill me himself!" She pointed toward the door. "Now, get out of here. I'll send for you when it's safe."

"And if I don't hear from you, then should I assume it isn't?"

She stared at him, her chest aching at his naiveté. "My boy, if you don't hear from me, then I'll be dead, and I'd highly recommend you never show your face in Paris again."

Fromont Residence
Paris, Kingdom of France

"Why don't you start at the beginning?"

Mr. Fromont nodded, still pale from the shock of his wife bringing a Templar Knight and his sergeant home with her. "I, umm, don't want to get anyone in trouble."

"Of course you don't, but trust me when I say, people are already in trouble. As I said to your wife, if we knew the motivations behind what has happened, perhaps we can avoid some of the unpleasantness that might be necessary."

"Y-you mean, umm, arrest?"

"I mean death, sir."

Fromont's eyes bulged, his wife yelping as she rushed to his side, gripping his arm. "You mean we might be executed?"

Marcus pointed toward the chair he assumed was the regular perch of the man. "Why don't we all sit down and discuss this calmly and thoroughly, shall we?"

Fromont shook out a nod, then sat, his wife standing dutifully by his side, gripping his shoulder, while Marcus and Simon took two chairs from the dining table and sat facing them.

Marcus put on his best smile. "Now, from the beginning, what is your involvement in this?"

Fromont paled further. "We're not involved. Not really."

Marcus leaned forward. "But?"

Fromont sighed. "But we have, I suppose, benefited."

"In what way?"

"We've used several of René's Letters of Credit to get ourselves out of debt to a most vile man."

"Pequin?"

Fromont's eyes bulged. "Yes! How did you know?"

"Your description is most apt, and we know he's involved." Marcus leaned back, hoping to put the Fromonts at ease. "Now, René has been creating forged Letters of Credit, and you have been redeeming them at Templar outposts around the city, is that correct?"

He nodded. "Yes, but not just us. Others have as well."

"Many?"

He shrugged. "I don't know, but there's talk. René was just trying to help. He wasn't being greedy. He's not a thief. He's a good man."

"I have no doubt, though what he has done is still a crime."

"I-I suppose. Though if his motives were pure, could you perhaps forgive him if he promised to never do it again?"

Marcus folded his arms. "We would need to talk to him first, to hear his side of things, before there's any chance of that."

"Oh, I assure you, his motives were pure. He's doing it to try and save his sisters. They're all alone, you see. Their parents are dead, and the three of them are all each other have. The girls are too young to marry, and he's afraid what might happen if something tragic befell him."

Simon grunted. "Getting involved with someone like Pequin would seem unwise, then."

Fromont frowned. "I assure you, that wasn't by choice, nor was it his fault."

Marcus regarded him. "How can you be so sure?"

Fromont blushed, his chin dropping into his chest as he stared at his hands. "I'm afraid that was my fault." He raised his chin, staring at them earnestly. "I swear, they made me tell them! They beat me–"

"Savagely!" cried his wife.

"Yes, savagely. I could barely walk for days. I had no choice but to tell them how I got the money to pay the loan early. They would have killed me!"

Marcus dismissed the man's concerns with a wave of his hand. "Nobody would blame you for speaking under those circumstances. You should feel no shame for what you were forced to do." He scratched his beard. "So, René broke our code, started forging Letters of Credit for himself and his neighbors, all in an effort to help his sisters and to help good people like you get out from under the thumbs of people like Pequin."

"Yes, but René owed money as well. To that wretch Thibault."

Marcus exchanged a glance with his sergeant. "Simone."

"Yes!" Fromont paused. "How does a Templar Knight know a woman like that?"

"We've had dealings." He gestured at the world outside. "I got the distinct impression that many in the neighborhood know about René and his deeds."

Fromont frowned, diverting his eyes. "I'm afraid that's my fault too. I may have said something when I was drunk."

His wife smacked him on the back of the head. "You fool! Now look what you've done. I've told you I didn't want you drinking anymore. You always get yourself in trouble."

"It was just a harmless drink."

"Not so harmless if something happens to René because of it." She swung again, but he ducked.

"We need to find René before the wrong people do."

Fromont, still crouching to avoid his wife's right hand, shrugged. "I haven't seen him in at least a few days."

"It's our understanding he's left the city."

"Did he take his sisters?"

"No. Unfortunately, they've been kidnapped."

Both Fromonts gasped. "Have they been harmed?"

"We don't know."

"By whom?"

"Again, we don't know, though we have our suspicions. We've been told that a man who worked for Pequin, named Alain, might know where René is now. Any idea how we might find him?"

Fromont nodded. "I know who you're talking about, I do business with his father from time to time. He's not far from here."

"Can you show us?"

Fromont rose from his chair. "Absolutely."

Marcus and Simon rose, and Marcus held up a finger. "Before we leave, I have one thing to say for the benefit of both of you. Say *nothing* more of this matter, and should anyone ask you how you paid off your loan, it was definitely *not* with a forged Templar Letter of Credit. Understood?"

Both Fromonts paled, then replied in unison. "Yes, sir."

Outside St. Mandel, Kingdom of France

Every muscle in René's body was tense, a second risked glance confirming the man on horseback was still behind him, having passed the split in the road, bypassing the turn for Paris. It could be innocent, simply another traveler heading north. Yet it could be something more sinister, as he was certain he had seen this man before.

How can you be so sure?

The man was a good distance behind, and it was more likely his panicked mind had simply filled in the blur that should be the man's face with someone familiar, someone who scared him.

Lyon!

His mouth filled with bile as he realized that was exactly who it was. He didn't need a clear view of the man's face to know there could be no doubt.

They know!

His agreement was one redemption per week.

No more.

Yet he had done more than half a dozen over the past two days, and had more to do before he completed the circuit tomorrow.

But why hadn't they stopped him? If Lyon was here, he was here for a reason. And where was Alain? Those two were rarely seen apart.

Maybe he's gone to see Pequin, to find out what to do.

It made sense. If Lyon and Alain were told to follow him, they would have been tailing him since yesterday.

It meant they likely followed his unexpected departure from his home, and didn't know until his second redemption that he was up to something he shouldn't be. Alain would have been sent back to Paris to find out what to do, and Lyon would have kept following him, awaiting instructions.

And when those instructions arrived, it might be the end.

Though he somehow doubted it. He was the only one who could create the forgeries. They needed him.

They could hurt the girls.

They couldn't beat him. They risked damaging his hands or eyes. But they could punish Grace or Vivienne for what he had done.

And that was exactly why he was doing it. To get away, so they would never be threatened again.

Yet he had been caught.

What are you going to do about it?

What could he do about it? If Alain returned with instructions to bring him back to Paris, then Pequin would do whatever it was he was going to do. If he didn't, Lyon would keep following him, then he'd be captured when he returned to Paris regardless, unable to escape with his sisters.

Either way, his entire plan was a failure.

Unless he could lose Lyon somehow and make it back to Paris first. He could fetch his sisters and leave before anyone would know.

His heart nearly stopped at a thought.

If Alain went back for instructions, then they already know.

His stomach flipped. If they knew what he was doing, then they might have already taken his sisters, so he couldn't try anything when he returned.

His entire body began to shake when he heard a shout.

"You there, halt!"

Lyon cursed as the Templar Knight charged past him, shouting toward René ahead of him. There was little doubt now their scam had been discovered, and they knew exactly who was behind it.

René Courvat.

Exactly as Pequin had said.

He smiled slightly as René turned in his saddle, his jaw dropping at the sight of the knight, in full regalia, charging toward him. It was an impressive sight as a witness, and no doubt a terrifying one if the subject of the man's attention.

But now he faced a dilemma. If the Templars knew it was René, then everything was done. But was it? Did the Templars know, or did just this man know? And if it were just this man, then perhaps there was still hope to keep the scam alive.

René had to be saved. It was the only way for the scam to continue. And if *he* were the one to save the code breaker, then Pequin would be eternally grateful.

You'd be his number two.

He smiled at the prospect.

The money.

The power.

The women.

His smile turned into an outright lecherous grin.

The women.

He drew his sword and charged, no thought given

to the fact he was about to engage a Templar Knight with far more experience in battle than he could hope to match.

Damase cursed as his target bolted, though the choice to flee at least confirmed one thing.

It was his man.

Guilty men don't run from Templars.

He urged his horse forward when he cocked an ear, the sound of hoofbeats behind him unmistakable. He glanced over his shoulder to see the man he had passed moments before now charging him, his sword drawn.

He cursed.

Then debated what to do. If he stopped to engage the man, then he might lose his target, yet if he didn't, the man might still catch up to him, giving him no time to prepare himself.

And his shoulder was still smarting from his previous encounter with the Hospitallers.

Damn the Saracen who wounded me!

He had no choice.

He pulled up on his reins, turning his well-trained steed, and drew his sword. He again had to incapacitate his man quickly, for an extended swordfight would not go well for him—his arm would tire quickly, and he'd be forced to fight with his left, something he trained for, yet hadn't done in at least a year.

You should have kept with your training, you old fool!

Though perhaps diplomacy might be the order of the day.

"I am Sir Damase de Sissey, Templar Knight. I call on you to withdraw from this field of battle. There is no possible way you can win here today, and I have no desire to take your life."

The man continued his charge. "I am Lyon, and I don't give a shit who you are, have no intention of dying, and think I can easily whip an old man's ass."

Damase smiled slightly at the uncouth soul now mere feet away, and decided he should heed the young man's warning. He tossed his sword in the air, grabbing it with his left hand, then withdrew his dagger from his belt. Raising the sword over his head, he parried his opponent's attack, and as he did so, leaned to his right and buried the dagger in the man's stomach.

The young man cried out as Damase turned his horse to face the man should he attempt to engage again, though there was no risk of that. The man gripped his stomach, blood pouring over his hands from the wound, a wound that would be fatal within moments.

And painful.

He climbed off his horse and sheathed his sword, his opponent's clattering to the ground. He reached up and pulled the man off his horse and lay him gently on the road, staring into his eyes. "Easy now, it won't be long."

"Y-you killed me."

"I did, though I did offer you the option to withdraw."

The man's eyes flooded with tears as he paled. "I-I should have listened."

"Yes, you should have, but do not worry. You are in God's hands now."

The man stared up at him, fear in his eyes. "But I haven't been a good man. Heaven is no place for a soul like mine."

Damase patted him on the shoulder, smiling gently. "You would be surprised at the mercy our Lord is capable of. Let Him decide your fate, not your fears."

The man reached up and grabbed his arm. "Don't be harsh with René. We forced him to work for us."

Damase gripped the man's hand. "I shall show him the same mercy I hope the Lord shows you."

Something snapped behind him, a sound he recognized too well, and he cried out as the bolt from a crossbow pierced his back between his shoulder blades, its tip penetrating his heart, and he collapsed atop his opponent, his life rapidly coming to a close from the fatal wound, a smile spreading.

Thank you, Lord, for letting me die with honor, in battle.

His final breath sighed from his body.

And curse the man who would shoot another in the back.

Alain threw his crossbow aside, rushing toward his friend. He hauled the body of the Templar off Lyon, then stared down at him, unsure of what to do, the sight of so much blood churning his stomach.

He asked the only person he could.

"Wh-what should I do?"

Lyon shook his head slowly. "There's nothing you can do, but you've killed a Templar. You must run."

"To where? They k-killed them. They k-killed them all!"

"What do you mean?" Lyon's voice was weak, barely a whisper.

"Pequin, ev-everyone. They're all dead. Someone k-killed them all."

Lyon reached up, his hand clasping Alain's neck. "Then run, and never look back." The hand fell away, slapping onto the ground, Lyon's eyes staring up at Alain, no life left in them.

Alain fell back on his backside, sobbing, staring at his friend who had treated him so poorly, then at the knight who had killed him. A Christian monk.

You're going to burn in Hell.

His chest tightened.

And you're going to burn here *if they catch you.*

He scrambled to his feet, checking in both directions to make sure he was alone, then dragged the body of the Templar off the road and into the trees. He removed anything identifiable from the knight's horse, then smacked it on the ass, sending it on its way, farther away from Paris. He stared at the body of his friend, uncertain as to what to do. He wanted to take him home, back to his family, yet he couldn't be seen carrying a body.

Too many questions would be asked.

He decided to stash him in the woods as well, with plans to tell his family where to find him when things calmed down.

Yet he couldn't put him too close to the slain Templar, it would connect the two deaths, and could lead back to him, and a noose for certain.

He threw his friend's body over his horse, then led it a couple of miles down the road before dumping the body and covering it with underbrush. He said a silent prayer, then decided to ignore his friend's final advice to him, and instead return to his father's, the one man he trusted to tell him the right thing to do.

And he was terrified as to what that might be.

Juda shook his head. "Sir Gotfried isn't going to believe this."

Leonard agreed. "You have to admire the old guy, though. He took out the young one quite expertly." He pointed in the direction the man the knight had been pursuing had fled. "That has to be René Courvat. I can't see any other reason a Templar would be chasing him, or why an associate of Alain was following him. That must have been the Lyon guy Pequin mentioned."

"Must be."

"Sir Konrad was right. Waiting at the tavern in case Alain returned was the right move."

"We got lucky. I didn't think he'd be stupid enough to return."

Leonard shrugged. "Well, he didn't know what had happened, so it wasn't that unexpected. If something happened to you, wouldn't you try to get back to headquarters?"

Juda nodded, urging his horse forward and out of the forest they had hidden in as Alain took the road back toward Paris. "Let's catch up to this René character before he decides to leave the road and hide. I'd hate to tell Sir Gotfried that we had him then let him escape."

Leonard grunted. "If we lose him, I'm not saying a word to anybody."

Juda chuckled. "Good thinking." On the road, he smacked his steed, sending her surging forward. "But I'd rather just find him before having to break my vows."

Sir Gotfried's Headquarters
Paris, Kingdom of France

Grace sat huddled on the straw mattress tossed in the corner of the small, dark, damp room shortly after their unceremonious arrival. Her older sister was holding her tight, putting on a brave face, though her trembling gave away her fears.

A lone candle, held by her sister, cast a dull glow on the room, revealing little beyond the fact there were no windows here, no furniture, and simply a wooden door that had remained closed since they had been put in here.

On the other side, however, were sounds that continued to terrify. Voices, speaking a language she didn't understand, men marching past, back and forth, and the savage sounds of what had to be a man receiving the most vicious of beatings nearby, his cries both petrifying and heartbreaking.

It was all very confusing to her. She had always been taught that knights were honorable, that they were sworn to protect people like her, yet here they were, held prisoner yet again.

Though were they? Their situation seemed better than before, where that filthy Pequin had tried to have his way with her sister. She had seen the carnage at the tavern as they were led through it. It had been so horrifying, she had gone numb for several moments, her eyes squeezed shut, her breath held, her hands pressed against her ears, as she struggled to deprive her senses of the wretched feast presented to them.

And a small part of her was happy about what had happened.

For it must mean Pequin and those that had kidnapped them, that had terrorized them and their brother for months, were now dead.

These men had definitely treated them better. After they were outside the tavern, several of them in their black and white tunics and surcoats took them to wherever this place was. They had asked if they knew where René was, and when they said they didn't, they had been put in here and given the mattress.

"Do you think when they find René, they'll let us go?"

Vivienne flinched at her voice. "I don't know. I hope so."

"Are these men knights?"

"I think so."

"Then shouldn't they be men of honor?"

"That's what I always thought."

"Then why are we here?"

"Perhaps there's nowhere for us to go."

Grace's heart ached with a thought. "Do you think René is dead?"

Vivienne's chest heaved and she squeezed her sister tighter. "I pray that he isn't." She stifled a sob. "These men don't seem to think he is."

Grace's eyes narrowed. "Why do you say that?"

"If they thought he was dead, then they wouldn't have asked us where he was."

Grace's eyes widened. "I hadn't thought of that!"

The door opened and they both pushed deeper into the corner, their bodies pressed against the cold earthen walls.

A woman entered with a broad smile, holding up a tray with a candle and two steaming bowls of something. "You girls hungry?"

They were both too scared to answer.

The woman stepped inside and placed the tray beside them, revealing two bowls of a hearty stew. "You should eat. You've both been through a lot." She kneeled beside them. "Did those men, umm, do anything to you?"

Vivienne shook her head but Grace, with renewed hope her brother might be alive, was having none of that. "They tried with my sister, but she kicked that evil Pequin in the balls!"

The woman laughed hard, tossing her head back, and even Vivienne giggled, leaving Grace to still wonder why it was called balls, and why that was so funny.

"Well, your sister must be a good kicker to hit such a small target, from what I hear."

Grace was pleased even Vivienne was confused enough to mimic her response. "Huh?"

The woman smiled, patting them both on the shoulder. "Never you mind." She tapped the tray. "Now, you two eat up. You'll need your strength."

"When can we go home?" asked Vivienne.

"This will all be over once we find your brother."

Grace shivered. "Are you going to hurt him?"

"Why would you think a thing like that?"

"Because of what he did."

"What did he do?"

"He broke the code."

"Did he now?"

"Yes, and when the Templars find out, they're going to kill him."

"Well, you're under our protection now."

Grace wasn't convinced. "But aren't you on their side?"

"Why would you say that?"

"Because you're knights, just like the Templars."

The woman leaped to her feet and spat on the floor. "We're nothing like them!" She lowered her voice, calming down slightly. "And don't let any of the men hear you say such a dastardly thing! They'll beat you until you're black and blue, I assure you!"

She spun on her heel and left, closing the door behind her with a bang. Grace buried her head in her sister's chest, any doubt they were in a better place than before gone.

They weren't.

For how could anyone good hate the Templars so much?

Alain's Father's Residence
Paris, Kingdom of France

"That little imp has always been a thorn in my side. I swear his antics led my poor wife to an early grave."

The tirade against his son had been ongoing for the past short while, little opportunity provided for Marcus to get a word in edgewise.

Marcus glanced at Tanya and bared his teeth.

She growled back then barked, silencing Alain's father.

Marcus flashed her a smile and she barked again, her tail wagging.

"I understand Alain hasn't been the finest example of a good Christian, sir, however it is imperative that we find him. Surely, despite his misdeeds, you don't wish harm to come to him."

The man frowned, dropping into the lone seat in the workshop. "No, I suppose not. He is my son, and I still love him, no matter the disappointment he's become." He sighed. "And it's not really his fault. He's never been a smart one, that fool. I tried to teach him my trade so he could take over the shop one day, but he was just so uncoordinated, he kept either hurting himself or trying to burn down the place." He shook his head, staring into the distance. "My grandfather was a blacksmith, as was my father, myself, and now no one. We only ever had the one child. We prayed for more, but they never came." He stared up at the Templars. "So, what has my boy done this time?"

"There was an incident at the Shrieking Owl Tavern. Have you heard about it?"

He shook his head. "No, I've been working since I woke. Haven't spoken to anybody. Please tell me it burned to the ground, taking that bastard Pequin with it."

Marcus chuckled. "No, it didn't burn to the ground, though everyone inside it, including Pequin, was murdered."

The man jumped to his feet, grabbing Marcus by the shoulders. "My boy! Is he among them?"

Marcus took him by the arms and directed him back to his seat. "No, though the men who committed this atrocity are looking for him. If you know anything, tell us now so that we might help him."

The man wiped tears from his eyes, then stared up at them. "What do you want with him?"

"We're hoping he knows the whereabouts of someone we seek. I assure you, we have no interest in your son, however when we find him, we will put him under our protection until things get sorted out."

The man drew a deep breath then exhaled loudly. "Very well. He was here very early this morning. He said he needed a horse. I gave him one. He said he'd be back by tomorrow with it."

"Did he say where he was going?"

The man shook his head. "No, just that he was heading east, about a half day's ride."

Marcus suppressed a smile. Half a day's ride east of here was the general vicinity of where Damase was supposed to be. It couldn't be a coincidence. "Did he say who he was meeting?"

"No, just a friend. Business related. He didn't get

into it, but he did seem scared." His shoulders slumped. "If I had known what had happened, I would have told him to keep riding and never come back." He looked up, his eyes bloodshot. "Is my boy in trouble?"

Marcus kneeled in front of the concerned father. "He might be. I'll tell you all I know, though I must warn you, some of it is hearsay. We spoke to Mr. Pequin just before he died. He claimed Hospitallers had committed the massacre, and that they were now looking for your son, because Pequin told them he might know where Mr. René Courvat might be. There are reports that it was these same Hospitallers that were after your son last night, and that he escaped. Do you know Mr. Courvat?"

"Of him, yes." The man hesitated. "There are, umm, rumors going about that he, well, umm, perhaps I shouldn't say."

"That he's broken our code?"

The man's eyes bulged. "Yes! You know?"

Marcus chose to not confirm anything. "We know of the rumors, yes."

"So, it's true?"

Marcus shook his head. "I definitely didn't say *that*."

The man gave him a look. "Would you admit to it if it were true?"

Marcus laughed. "Probably not!"

"So, it's hogwash?"

Marcus smiled. "I fear it's as simple as Mr. Courvat coming into some money, and using it to help his friends and neighbors, providing them with a tall tale to go along with it. The Templar code is unbreakable, I assure you. It has stood unbroken for over a century, and will remain so for another, I'm certain."

"Of course, of course. I should know better than to waste my time on fanciful tales." He paused. "But someone obviously believes it, don't you think?"

"Why?"

"Well, these Hospitallers killing all those people and trying to kill my son. They must believe it. And it's not exactly a secret that you, I mean the Templars, and the Hospitallers aren't exactly on friendly terms. And Pequin was a known loan shark and an all-around bad sort. Hospitallers wouldn't kill them for no reason."

Marcus said nothing in the hopes the man might reveal something he didn't already know.

The man continued. "What I heard was that René was forging Templar Letters of Credit, and people were using them to pay off their debts. A man like that wouldn't be too happy at losing out on all that interest."

Marcus nodded. "If what you say is true, then I would agree." He glanced at the door. "Should your son return, have him report to the Templar fortress and ask for me. I shall try to help him as best I can. If indeed Hospitallers are after him, we may be the only ones who can protect him."

The man rose and grasped Marcus' hands. "Thank you, sir, you are a good man."

Marcus bid their adieu and left the blacksmith's shop, Simon and Tanya in tow.

Simon cleared his throat as he mounted his horse. "So, what do you make of that?"

Marcus frowned, looking about. "I think half this neighborhood knows our code has been broken, and if we don't shut down these rumors soon, it might not matter what happens with Mr. Courvat. It could already be too late."

Outside St. Mandel, Kingdom of France

Christoffle's feet were aching from the daily walks, but the pain was worth it.

He loved her.

And she loved him.

And they would marry one day, one day soon. He still hadn't asked her. He was too shy, and they were still too young, though he was certain she knew he wanted to. When the time was right, he'd ask permission of her father, and once the blessing was received, he would formally ask her, on his knee, her hands in his.

And if he knew her heart, as he hoped he did, she would say yes, and they would be forever one.

He couldn't wait.

Nothing could come between them, for at this very moment, his life was perfect. His parents had already indicated their blessing for the potential union, and his father had offered them half the family farm to start their life on, where they would build their own home, raise a family, and live happily ever after.

So long as nothing screwed things up.

Like permanently damaged feet.

He stared at his worn shoes.

Curse these things!

His dog barked and bolted into the woods, after some small animal, he was sure. "Get back here! Now!"

A bark from inside the dark forest was the response, yet the mutt didn't return.

"I said, get back here!"

Again a bark, this one sounding distressed.

He bolted after him, reaching for his dagger, fearing the worst.

And finding it.

"Get back!" he ordered, pushing his faithful companion away from a body covered in leaves. He gingerly brushed aside some of the brush covering the man and gasped when the bright red cross on a crisp white background was revealed. "A Templar!"

His shoulders slumped as he fell backward.

Of all the things to find!

Courvat Residence
Paris, Kingdom of France

"Vivienne! Grace! Where are you?"

René rushed up the stairs, the ground floor empty, his heart hammering with trepidation as what he was sure to find on the second floor.

Nothing.

They were gone.

He collapsed to his knees, grabbing at his hair as he struggled to control the sobs that threatened to overwhelm him.

They're not dead.

Though that wasn't necessarily true. All he could say for certain was that they hadn't been killed here. He rose, carefully looking about for any clues as to what had happened, and found none. A surge of hope shot through him and he dropped to his knees again, peering under the bed.

And found nothing, his hope fading as rapidly as it had come.

He made a thorough but futile search of the upstairs in case the girls were hiding, continually calling their names, then returned to the ground floor, where it was clear a struggle had taken place, furniture overturned, a jar shattered against the wall, and two plates of uneaten food sitting on the table, rats making a feast of it.

He shuddered at the sight of them, and made to do something about it when he turned for the door.

There was no time to waste on rats.

Someone had his sisters, and he suspected who. It had to be Pequin. Lyon wouldn't have been alone, which meant Alain or someone else had reported to Pequin what he was up to, and his sisters had been taken as punishment.

Oh God, please let them still be undefiled!

He rushed outside and spotted one of his neighbors. "Do you know where my sisters are?"

She frowned, and his worst fears were confirmed. "I'm afraid Pequin has them. They took them last night."

René didn't bother letting her finish, instead mounting his borrowed horse, the poor beast exhausted from his hours long rush home, and raced for the tavern that served as Pequin's home and place of business.

A place where untold depravities occurred.

If he's touched my sisters, Lord, give me the strength to kill him. I don't care what happens to me, just let me kill him!

He gasped as he turned a corner, certain the Lord would never look kindly upon such a prayer, then doubting his doubts as he took in the sight ahead. What appeared to be at least a dozen bodies were lying on the ground outside the Shrieking Owl Tavern, and more were still being brought out.

He dismounted, then smiled at the sight of Pequin, gored and dead, lying on the street in the mud.

Then his heart leaped into his throat and he rushed forward. "My sisters! Are they in there?"

Nobody paid him any mind, all continuing in their grim task. He spotted the parish priest and dropped to his knees in front of him. "Please, Father, are my sisters inside? Are they part of this tragedy?"

The man smiled at him, placing a gentle hand on his shoulder. "No, my dear René, they aren't."

René slumped and he wept with relief. "Oh, thank God!" He struggled to his feet. "Wh-what happened here?"

"We're not exactly sure. Rumor has it that Hospitallers did this, but I somehow doubt it. They're Christian knights. They wouldn't do such a thing."

René had to agree, though the good Father didn't know what he did, didn't know about the broken Templar code, something the Hospitallers would stop at nothing to possess.

"Why do you think your sisters might be here?"

"My neighbors said they had been taken by Pequin's men last night."

The priest frowned. "Well, I'm not sure why he would do such a thing, however I can assure you they aren't here."

René clasped his hands behind his head, spinning in circles. "Then where could they be?"

"Well, my son, if they were here, and no longer are, then I would suggest whoever did this now has them."

René threw his head back, staring up at the heavens. "Oh no! What am I going to do!" He stared at the priest. "If Hospitallers have them, there's no hope!"

The priest shook his head. "Nonsense, my son. Like I said, I find it impossible to believe that Christian knights had anything to do with this." René was about to open his mouth to protest when he was stopped with a finger held in front of his face. "However, there might be someone who can help you. Apparently, there were two Templars here asking questions. I am certain you can trust them, and that they too are seeking the truth of what happened. Find them, and perhaps they can help you find your sisters."

René shook all over at the very idea. There was only one reason Templars were here, and it wasn't to find those responsible for the massacre, but to find him. Yet he couldn't tell the priest that. "Wh-where might I find them?"

"I don't know, though I think I heard someone say they were looking for that imp Alain. Apparently, he was chased out of his room last night by these same people."

"Thank you, Father." René mounted his horse and turned it around, heading for the one place he could think of where Alain might be hiding.

His father's blacksmith shop.

Enclos du Temple, Templar Fortress
Paris, Kingdom of France

Sir Matthew Norris slammed his fist onto his desk, everything on it jumping then crashing down in protest. The messenger who had brought the bad news leaped forward, righting a candle before it could do any damage, then withdrew lest another fist be thrust into action.

Matthew jabbed a finger at him. "I want a meeting with that Hospitaller bastard right away! Tonight!"

The messenger bowed. "Yes, sir."

"And get word to Sir Marcus. Tell him about Sir Damase."

"At once, sir."

Matthew dismissed the man with a flick of the wrist then collapsed back in his chair. Damase. Dead. Shot in the back by a crossbow outside St. Mandel, and evidently shortly after an altercation with two Hospitallers, one of whom Damase killed. The incidents had to be connected, especially with the report from Marcus suggesting Hospitallers might be aware of the broken code, since they massacred over two dozen last night while searching for the code breaker.

It was madness.

And it was the worst case scenario coming true.

Damase had been right.

If the wrong people got wind of what had happened, it could destroy the Order.

And the Hospitallers were the worst possible people to have found out.

He had to put an end to this now, though he wasn't sure how. There was no proof Hospitallers had killed Damase. There were no witnesses to either altercation, at least none that had come forward. They only had Damase's word with respect to the initial encounter, though he had no doubt as to its veracity. After all, Damase was a Templar Knight, and would never lie.

But none of that mattered. If the Hospitallers knew the code had been broken, then it was already too late.

They had to find the man mentioned in Marcus' report. This René Courvat. They had to put an end to his mischief, then quash any knowledge of his accomplishment.

We need to spread rumors that it was all a lie.

He smiled slightly, his pounding heart calming slightly as a plan slowly came together. If they could capture the code breaker, perhaps they could force him to tell the story they wanted put out there. Use the guilty man, rather than just kill him. Create a disinformation campaign that would contradict the rumors, but give a perfectly plausible explanation as to why there were people out there who thought differently.

He'd have to come up with all those explanations quickly, for if he didn't, no amount of contradictory rumors would stop what was already out there.

Especially if Hospitallers were behind this.

He slammed his fist against his desk. "Damned Hospitallers!"

Someone yelped in the shadows and Matthew leaped to his feet. "Who goes there?"

One of the stable boys emerged. "It's just me, sir."

"What the Devil are you doing here?"

"Just waiting for something to do, sir."

"If you're looking for something other than a hide tanning, then get out of here. I'm sure there are stables to be cleaned."

"Yes, sir!" The boy bolted out the door and Matthew returned to his seat and his thoughts.

He tapped his chin, the brief interruption allowing every road his mind had traveled to return to the starting point.

Why was Damase killed?

If it were indeed Hospitallers, then there was only one reason to kill him—he must have discovered who the code breaker was, and they didn't want that information coming back here. Yet if that were the case, then the Hospitallers would not only need to have known about the code—which according to Marcus' latest update, they did at least as early as late last night—but they would have had to know Damase was investigating the matter.

And almost no one knew that.

His jaw sagged slowly.

We have a spy!

En route to St. Mandel, Kingdom of France

"Greetings, my fellow Templars!"

Marcus turned in his saddle to see a Templar messenger galloping toward them, his hand held high. He turned to face him, as did Simon and a growling Tanya. "Sit, girl."

She did, though her teeth continued to be bared.

The messenger came to a halt, gasping for breath. "Would you be by chance Sir Marcus de Rancourt?"

"I am."

"Oh, thank the good Lord! I have an urgent message for you from Sir Matthew Norris." He produced a document and handed it over. Marcus snapped the seal and unfolded the paper, quickly reading its contents, his heart aching at what he read.

"What's wrong?" asked Simon, detecting his pain as only a good friend could.

"Sir Damase is dead."

"What? By whose hand?"

"Hospitallers are suspected. Apparently, he had an encounter with them earlier and killed one of them."

Simon cursed. "First they kill everyone in that tavern, then Damase? What are they thinking?"

"I'm not sure what's going on. It says here the body has been taken to St. Mandel. That's where his last dispatch said he was, so let's continue there as planned."

"For what purpose? Revenge?"

"No, to see if he had any papers with him that might

be of importance, and if anybody saw anything, especially Hospitallers."

Simon growled, Tanya joining in. "I'd like my sword to taste Hospitaller blood for this."

Marcus shook his head. "Not today, not unless confronted. I don't want to jump to any conclusions. One altercation doesn't necessarily mean the second was connected."

"You think it's just a coincidence?" Simon apparently wasn't convinced.

Marcus frowned, eying the fading light. "I don't know what to think, but I'd like to find out before dusk."

De Rancourt Residence
Crécy-la-Chapelle, Kingdom of France

"Thomas, is that you?"

Thomas smiled and waved at Jeremy then David, both dropping their farming implements and rushing down the gentle slope toward him. He dismounted and stretched, his entire body aching from the hours-long ride from the great city to the west. He wasn't used to riding a horse, let alone riding one for so long, and he'd be paying for it even more so tomorrow when he woke.

"It's so good to see you!" David extended a filthy hand and Thomas eyed it. The squire, at least a decade his senior, withdrew it. "Sorry, forgot myself there. What brings you here?"

"It's a bit of a story that."

"And it's one I'd like to hear." They all turned to see Lady Joanne standing in the doorway of the farmhouse, her hands on her hips. "Well, don't just stand there, boy, give me a hug!"

She held out her arms and Thomas smiled. Jeremy took the reins of his horse and he strode quickly to the welcoming arms of a woman who barely knew him, yet treated him like a son. She hugged him hard and he closed his eyes, picturing his own mother embracing him in his youth, and his eyes burned with how much he missed how safe he always felt in her arms.

Joanne let him go then held him out, her fingers flicking through his hair as she attempted to make him presentable. "Forget it. Get inside, wash up, and I'll send for Isabelle. She'll be so thrilled to know you're here."

He blushed and nodded, heading inside, Beatrice rushing over and grabbing him, smushing his head into her impressive bosom. She grinned at him then pushed him toward the rear of the small home where he could wash up. He made as quick work of it as possible, the shouts outside suggesting Jeremy had been sent to inform Isabelle, the evening meal was being upgraded in his honor, and apparently his arrival was not to be used as an excuse for neglecting farm work, despite the late hour.

As he finished, he peered out the window to see David, Jeremy, Jacques, and Pierre all toiling away in the fading light, harder at work than he had been in some time. He used to try and get shifts at the docks along the river, unloading and loading goods for transport along the mighty waterway, but work was always hard to come by, and muscled men were preferred.

Like here.

Even young Pierre appeared to be bulking up and could probably beat him in a fight.

He squeezed his skinny arm, frowning.

Once Isabelle sees you as the day you were born, she's going to realize you're no man.

"Thomas! Where are you?"

His heart skipped a beat at the sound of her voice, then raced with excitement as his stomach flipped. He always felt oddly unsettled around her and wasn't sure why. Was it love? Or was it something else? He had never been in love before, so it was all still new to him. And he had no one to advise him. His parents were gone, he had no siblings, he couldn't talk to his coworkers about it, though he had a sense lately that perhaps Simone wasn't as coldhearted as she made herself out to be—and anything Enzo said beyond a grunt would be unhelpful. Then there were his only friends, these Templars, all sworn to celibacy, so what did they know of love?

He had no one.

Except Isabelle.

He checked himself for presentability then returned to the front of the house, unable to suppress his smile at the sight of Isabelle. She rushed into his arms and hugged him hard, then planted a kiss on him that had the entire room in genuine jubilation.

And his cheeks as red as apples.

"Why are you here?" asked Isabelle, leading him to a chair at the table. He sat, the others filling the remaining seats, even David and Jeremy apparently given a reprieve by their taskmaster.

"Mrs. Thibault sent me."

Isabelle eyed him. "Really? Whatever for?"

He wasn't sure what he should say, if anything. The situation was dangerous, and he didn't want to put Isabelle or the others at risk, yet if he couldn't tell these people, who could he tell? David and Jeremy, he wasn't worried about. He had seen them in battle and they would be eager to help. It was the women and children that concerned him, though if he were to suggest it, the women of this household would take him down a peg or two for it.

He sighed, his shoulders slumping. "Very well, I'll tell you everything, but what I tell you must remain among ourselves." He glanced at the children then at Joanne. "It cannot be repeated to anyone."

Joanne rose. "Say no more. Children, outside, now, and don't let me catch you listening at the window, or there will be hell to pay!"

Awws and stomped feet were the response, but moments later there was laughter as the chase was on outside. Joanne returned to her seat as Beatrice served a freshly brewed tisane. "Tell us what's going on, Thomas."

Isabelle took his hand and squeezed it, injecting some courage. He smiled weakly at her.

"Very well, here's what I know. Someone has broken the Templar code—"

"You know about that?" interrupted Jeremy. "How?"

"Let the poor boy speak, and maybe he'll tell us!" growled Beatrice.

Jeremy lowered his head. "Sorry."

Thomas smiled slightly. "Well, a man named René owed Mrs. Thibault money, and he paid it back early. Then another loan shark named Pequin was dressing a little too fine for her liking, so she got suspicious something was going on. She had me and Enzo get one of his men drunk, and he told us that René had broken the code and was using it to forge Templar Letters of Credit."

"Sir Damase was right!" David belted Jeremy on the shoulder. "I win. You shovel my shit tomorrow."

Thomas thought the idea horrifying and carried on. "When Mrs. Thibault found out, she got excited, but wouldn't tell me why. All I know is she had a series of secret meetings with someone, and claimed it was going to change everything. Then she got scared and told me to come here until I heard from her, and she said that if I didn't, she was probably dead, and I should never show my face in Paris again."

Isabelle rested her head on his shoulder, gripping his arm. "That sounds like a wonderful idea."

David ignored her. "Does she really think things are that dangerous?"

"She does. She seemed genuinely scared. I don't recall ever seeing her that frightened or uncertain."

"And Sir Marcus? What news do you have of him?"

"Only that they were planning on rendezvousing with someone, I can't remember his name."

"Sir Damase de Sissey?"

Thomas' eyes widened. "Yes, that's it! But when I told them what I knew, they changed their plans and decided to seek out René first. From there, I don't know what became of them, but if Mrs. Thibault is scared, I fear they might be in danger as well."

David rose. "That's it, we're leaving. We can be in Paris by morning if we travel by moonlight."

Joanne wagged a finger. "It's only a half moon."

David headed for the door. "A moon is a moon when the sky is clear, which it is. We can't wait until morning."

Joanne was having none of it. "And just how do you plan on finding them? Paris is a big city, and you don't even know if they're in it."

"The fortress might know, and if not, we'll start at this René's house. Someone will have seen them. We'll just follow their trail." He frowned. "I wish we had Tanya. That girl can sniff out anyone."

Jeremy joined him by the door. "Well, we don't. We'll have to rely on God to guide us." He grinned.

"Let's just hope He's not too busy."

"Do you want me to come with you?" Thomas couldn't believe the words he had heard came from his own mouth.

David stared at him, apparently impressed with the offer. "It would make things much easier. You know the area far better than we do."

Isabelle squeezed his arm tighter. "No, don't take him. It's too dangerous, and he's not a soldier like you!"

"We can protect him."

Isabelle squeezed tighter. "Can you guarantee his safety?"

David paused, then shook his head. "No, of course not. But Thomas can ride a horse, which means he can retreat should we encounter danger. But we need to find Sir Marcus. He'll need our skills should there be someone out there more powerful than a clever man who discovered how to crack our code. With what you've told us, Master Thomas, something more sinister is going on if someone like Mrs. Thibault is scared, and I'm afraid Sir Marcus doesn't realize it."

Thomas looked at Isabelle, putting on a brave smile for her, though the shaking of his body betrayed his fear. "It's fine. They're right. I know the area, I know the people involved. I can help."

"But Mrs. Thibault told you not to return until she sent word."

"Yes, but Sir Marcus saved my life, and yours. We both owe it to him."

She sighed, dropping her forehead onto his shoulder. "You're right, of course." She stared up at him, her eyes burning. "Please be careful!" She grabbed him, kissing him hard, and by the time he came up for air, he was seeing stars, and grinning faces.

Isabelle turned on the two squires, jabbing a finger at them both. "If anything happens to him, you'll answer to me!"

David bowed deeply. "Yes, ma'am." The two filthy men beat a hasty retreat for their barracks and Thomas followed once he extricated himself from Isabelle's clinging embrace. He found the two squires equipping three fresh horses, his own already in the barn and stripped down, apparently while he conducted his ablutions while waiting for Isabelle's arrival.

As David worked, he belted out instructions to Thomas as if he were a raw recruit just joining the Order. "You listen to every word I say. If I tell you to run away, you run. I don't want to be the one to tell that lovely girl down there that you got killed."

Jeremy paused. "You're afraid of her?"

David eyed him. "Aren't you?"

"Terrified." Jeremy smacked Thomas on the back. "But don't worry, I'm sure she'll make a great wife!"

David grinned. "Just don't cross her. She'll kick your ass!"

Thomas gulped. "I don't doubt it." His heart nearly stopped and his eyes bulged. "Wife? Has she, umm, said anything?"

Both squires stopped, David finally laughing. "My boy, she's an unwed young woman in love. She talks of nothing but!"

"Which is a huge relief to Sir Marcus, now that he's no longer the subject of her affections," added Jeremy.

"Yes, you better marry that woman soon, before she thinks you're not interested." David's eyes narrowed, evidently picking up on Thomas' body language. "You *are* interested, aren't you?"

"I-I suppose."

"Suppose?" Jeremy stared at him incredulously. "What's to be supposing about? She's beautiful, loves you, is a wonderful cook, and keeps a good house. There's not a man in this town who wouldn't want her as his wife."

"But she'll never live in the city."

David frowned. "It doesn't sound like the city is exactly a great place to live." He took a gentler tone. "Look, life on the farm is hard, but it's rewarding. We have a great family here. Even the children are growing on me. And there's plenty of land for you and Isabelle to build your own home and start a family."

Thomas' shoulders sagged. "I'm not exactly built for farming. I've always been one to use my brains rather than my nonexistent brawn."

David took him by the shoulder, giving it a squeeze. "You're a man, and don't kid yourself, you've put on some meat since we saw you last."

Thomas grunted. "Being able to afford to eat does wonders."

Jeremy laughed. "There's always plenty to eat here. And by the end of the season, you'll have some bulk on those bones."

"But what of my skills? I really enjoy working with numbers, though not whom I'm doing it for."

David resumed prepping the horses. "Perhaps there's something you can do for the King or the Order. I'm sure Sir Marcus can figure something out." He inspected the horse, Jeremy doing the same with the others, then nodded with satisfaction. "Good. We're ready. We'll have plenty of time to talk along the way.

Who knows? By the time we get to Paris, we may have all your problems solved and your entire life planned out for you."

Thomas grunted. "That's what I'm afraid of."

Templar Outpost
St. Mandel, Kingdom of France

"There's no honor here."

Simon agreed with his master's assessment. "Exactly what you'd expect from a Hospitaller."

Marcus picked up the crossbow bolt that had penetrated his friend's back, now sitting on the table his body lay upon. "Where was he found?"

The knight in charge of the outpost stepped over to the wall where a map of the area hung. He pointed. "Not far out of town, as you can see. We think the body was dragged into the forest. It was only found because a man's dog caught the scent. We found his horse not much farther down the road, grazing."

"Papers? Messages?"

He pointed at another table. "All in the saddlebags. Whoever did this only stripped the horse of anything superficially indicating it belonged to a Templar."

Marcus retrieved the papers and found a map, various X's indicating a series of outposts and commanderies around the city, a route traced out. He also found a list of transactions, many of them marked, the towns they took place in matching those on the map. "It would appear he found a pattern by the looks of these transactions he's highlighted. It would appear he was retracing them, but in reverse. He must have been hoping to intercept someone."

"Oh, he found who he was looking for."

Marcus spun. "What?"

"Yes, it was quite a coincidence. The man he was looking for was here, redeemed a Letter of Credit, then had a brief interaction with Sir Damase as he was leaving. Something about a stomach bug, I believe."

"Describe the man."

"It would be better to read my official description." He flipped through the papers, finding the one he was seeking. He pointed at one of the entries. "Here."

Marcus read the brief description, and it generally matched what he had been told of René. He pursed his lips, staring at the map on the wall and where the body had been found. His eyebrows rose slightly. "He reversed course."

Simon looked at him. "What?"

"He went north. He was going in reverse, clockwise around the city. So, he should have gone south when he left here. Instead, he went north, which would be the direction René would go if he were continuing on his circuit around the city, counterclockwise."

Simon paused. "You don't think René killed him."

Marcus shrugged. "I don't know. From what we know of the man, he doesn't sound violent, but when confronted, who knows what a man is capable of."

"But he was shot in the back. If Damase was pursuing him and caught up to him, I doubt an experienced knight like him would have given him the opportunity."

Marcus agreed. "You're right, of course." He turned back to look at his slain friend. "No, a second person was involved here." He stepped over to the table and picked up the sword. "There's blood on this. Fresh. He was in an altercation with someone at close quarters, so it's highly unlikely that person would be engaging him with a crossbow, and doing so after blood was drawn, with Damase's back exposed. Look how far into the blade the blood goes. This sliced a man deeply." He turned to the outpost commander. "Was another body found?"

The man shook his head. "No." He eyed him. "What's this all about?"

"I can't say."

He frowned. "You sound just like him. He wouldn't tell me anything either."

Marcus smiled slightly. "I'm afraid secrecy is a necessity." He turned toward the map. "We should go to the location where he was found, then search the area."

The knight nodded toward the window. "Not until morning. You'll see nothing at this time of night. You could walk past a mass grave and miss it."

Marcus frowned, but had to agree. "We'll need quarters for two, and our dog tended to."

"And fresh horses and supplies in the morning, I assume?"

"Yes."

"Consider it done. "Now, let me show you to your quarters. It's past the dinner hour, but I'll try to arrange some food for you."

Simon's stomach growled and Tanya whimpered in response.

Marcus chuckled. "You better make it fast, otherwise these two might make a meal out of you."

Sir Gotfried's Headquarters
Paris, Kingdom of France

"That Templar investigator, he's dead."

Gotfried sat behind his desk, staring at the filthy little boy, one of their spies within the Templar ranks, and one who had proven to be quite resourceful. "Do you know his name?"

The boy nodded. "Sir Damase."

"How did he die?"

"Hospitallers. They killed him outside some place, umm, what was it, umm, oh! St. Mandel."

Gotfried pursed his lips, exchanging a glance with Konrad, standing in the corner. "If they believe that, then Sir Matthew must be quite upset."

The boy's eyes bulged. "He is that! He's demanded a meeting with the, umm, what do you call it?"

"Prior?"

"That's it!" The boy scratched at his opposite cheek. "Umm, there was something else." His eyes widened. "Oh yes! They also know what the guy looks like, that code breaker guy."

"Do they know his name yet?"

The boy shrugged. "I don't know. I don't think so."

Gotfried smiled. "Good. Then we know more than they do."

"Oh, and they mentioned Sir Marcus again."

"With respect to?"

"Umm, they sent him a message telling him about that guy's death, Damase."

Gotfried smiled at Konrad. "Then I think we know where to find him tomorrow." He turned back to the boy. "You're doing good work, son. Keep it up, and you'll soon be a squire in an honorable order, rather than a shit-shoveler in a den of ill repute." He jerked his chin toward the door. "Now go."

The boy bolted from the room and Konrad took his place in front of the desk. "What are your orders?"

"We continue with the original plan and expand upon it."

"How?"

"It seems clear that if we play this right, we can accomplish far more than we originally intended."

Konrad smiled. "Do you think it could work?"

"It has so far." He leaned back. "There's only one man I can see messing this up now, and that's Sir Marcus. He's been a thorn in our side before." He sat upright, his decision made. "Send a contingent to St. Mandel in the morning. Eliminate him and anyone with him." He smiled. "And make sure everyone knows who did it."

Alain's Father's Residence
Paris, Kingdom of France

"Who goes there?"

Alain held up his hands in the dark. "F-father, it's me."

There was a grunt then a candle was lit, his father revealed in his nightclothes, a grim expression framed by the feeble light. "You're back early."

Alain frowned. "Yes." He sighed, his shoulders slumping. "Father, I've d-done something horrible."

His father sat in his favorite chair, gesturing for Alain to sit in the seat closest. "What is it you've done this time?"

"I've, umm, k-killed a Templar Knight."

His father's eyes bulged. "Why would you do such a thing?"

"He had j-just killed Lyon. What-what was I supposed to do?"

"Lyon was a cretin, a piece of human garbage that worked for Pequin. The Templar was a monk, serving His Holiness in Rome, and the Lord Himself! You let him go about his business, that's what you do!"

Alain slumped in the chair. His father was right about everything, though he was missing one crucial point. "Lyon was my fr-friend."

His father spat. "No, he wasn't. None of them are, my boy. They tolerate you because they use you. You're the strongest boy I know. It comes from working the iron for all those years." He sighed. "I only wish you could have managed to coordinate those two hands of yours. You'd have made a wonderful blacksmith."

Alain felt hollow. "I'm sorry I f-failed you, Father."

His father rose and stepped closer, putting a hand on his shoulder. "It's not your fault, boy. It never was. You have nothing to be ashamed about. God made you who you are, and He had a purpose. He always does."

Alain burst into tears, the rare moment of tenderness from his father something he had needed desperately for so many years. "I h-hate being so stupid. My-my mouth is stupid, my-my eyes are stu-stupid. I can't do anything r-right." He rose and his father embraced him as his sobs continued, all the pain from all the years of torment releasing at once, and as he slowly calmed, he realized there was only one thing he could do to make things right.

And perhaps, end his suffering.

"I have t-to turn myself in."

His father pushed him away, maintaining his grip on his shoulders. "I've never been more proud of you than I am now."

A surge of satisfaction rushed through his body. "Th-thank you, Father."

"But I don't want you to. They'll kill you."

"I hope they do."

They both spun toward the voice in the darkness, and a shadow emerged into the candlelight.

It was René.

With a knife in his hand.

"René? What are y-you doing h-here?"

"Where are my sisters?"

Alain's eyes bulged. "I-I don't know. P-Pequin had

them, but-but he's dead."

His father stepped forward. "Now, René, son, just calm down. Nobody needs to get hurt here."

"Then tell me where my sisters are!"

The door kicked open, a sliver of moonlight highlighting the entry of four men, swords drawn, Hospitaller tunics proudly on display. "We have them."

René dropped the knife and Alain put himself between the new arrivals and his father. "Wh-what do you want?"

One of the men stepped forward. "You're all coming with us."

Alain held his arms out to his sides, blocking their path to his father. "We-we'll come, b-but not my father. He-he has nothing to do with th-this."

The knight agreed. "You're right, he doesn't." He shoved him to the side and plunged his blade deep in Alain's father's stomach. He sneered. "He can stay here."

Alain cried out, rushing to his father's side and catching him before he collapsed, then gently lowered him to the floor. "I-I'm so sorry, Father."

His father reached up and cupped his cheek. "It's not your fault, my boy."

"What sh-should I do?"

A tear rolled from his father's eye. "Survive."

Alain nodded, his heart aching as his father drew his final breaths, then passed with a shudder.

Then he erupted.

He surged toward the murderer and belted him in the chin, dropping the man with one blow. The other three rushed him, swords leading the way, but Alain didn't care. He was seeing red. He dropped atop his victim and rained blow after blow on him before something hit him from behind, the world slowly going dark as the roles reversed, and the blows pummeled him instead.

Sir Gotfried's Headquarters
Paris, Kingdom of France

"You understand your instructions?"

Simone trembled in her chair, already terrified by her late night summoning, and now even more so with what she had just been told. A bead of sweat raced down her back as she stared at Gotfried behind his desk, and it was but the first of many. "Y-yes." She could hear the fear in her voice. There was no disguising it, and Gotfried appeared to take great pleasure in her discomfort.

Yet despite her fear, it was also a time of jubilation. What she had hoped for was coming true. Her late husband's debt had been written off. She had the document to prove it. Evidently, Gotfried agreed her information had been valuable.

Invaluable.

Yet now she was pressed into service to exploit the information she had provided. And she dared not refuse.

"And they are?" prompted Gotfried, not convinced she was clear on them.

She drew a deep breath. "Starting tomorrow, my men and I will begin spreading the rumor that the Templar code has been broken, and that any payments being made using their Letters of Credit will be refused."

Gotfried leaned back. "Good. You have been listening."

She should have kept her mouth shut, but it wasn't her nature. "But, sir, I'm never paid in Letters of Credit. It doesn't make sense."

Gotfried shook his head as if at a child. "It doesn't matter. Just the fact that a respected"—she shifted in her chair from what she was sure was a backhanded compliment—"loan shark like you is refusing the Templars' Letters of Credit will be enough to make your entire community wonder what is going on. It will spread through Paris like wildfire, and soon those whispered rumors will reach the ears of the Court and the nobility that makes use of these Letters, and the job will be done. They will demand answers from the Templars, answers they cannot give without admitting that the code has been broken. And now that we have René, we will be able to prove it, should there be any doubt."

She tensed at the revelation René had been captured. She felt sorry for the man, though he had brought the situation upon himself. She forced a smile. "A brilliant plan."

"It is."

And again, she spoke without thinking. "And what do you expect to gain by it?"

It's none of your business! Stop asking questions! You have what you want!

Gotfried's smile turned into a sneer. "The destruction of the Templar Order."

She paled, all strength draining from her. "H-how?"

"Isn't it obvious? The source of their power is their wealth. The source of their wealth is their Letters of Credit, the collateral they hold, the fees they charge. It has made them far richer than most kingdoms, and it must be stopped."

"Why? Don't they serve a purpose?"

You really need to shut up!

Gotfried's face reddened. "Their actions are blasphemous! The Church forbids the charging of interest, yet they get around that by charging fees and collecting rent on held assets. They go against the word of God through their actions and must be stopped once and for all." He paused his tirade and stared at her. "Do you have a problem with what we're doing here?"

She gulped. "N-no. The Templars have never been my concern. Should they disappear tomorrow, I doubt I would even notice."

Gotfried relaxed, his cheeks returning to their normal pale white. "Good. Do your part, and you will be rewarded."

Her eyebrows rose, greed replacing fear. "Rewarded?"

"You upheld your end of the bargain by providing valuable information. You have been paid with the wiping of your husband's debt. Now, you will assist us with our plan, and you will be handsomely rewarded upon its success."

She couldn't help but smile. "Handsomely?"

Gotfried nodded. "Handsomely."

"And just how much is handsomely?"

You must stop!

"More than you could possibly imagine."

Her smile was a grin now. "I can imagine a lot."

"As can I." He leaned forward. "When we bring down the Templars, what do you think will happen?"

She shrugged, their downfall now a distant thought.

"I don't know. White tunics will go out of style?"

He chuckled. "Once this scandal spreads, the King will order them arrested, their assets seized. The King will know it was my order that is responsible for bringing this horrible situation to light, and we will be rewarded. And *you* will be rewarded." Her grin hurt. "Now, get out of here, and start spreading the word tomorrow."

She rose and bowed her way out of the room, then rushed home, any fear she might have had now overwhelmed by the greed of what was to come.

God bless that René!

Enclos du Temple, Templar Fortress
Paris, Kingdom of France

"How dare you summon me at this hour in such a manner!"

Sir Matthew Norris regarded his Hospitaller counterpart, Sir Bertrand de Montaigu, the disdain he felt for the man written on his face. "And yet you are here."

"Only because I just received news one of your knights killed one of my own."

"And then your men killed him!"

"Nonsense!"

"Nonsense? He was killed by a crossbow, shot in his back. Just the type of cowardly, dishonorable thing I would expect from a Hospitaller!"

Bertrand gripped the hilt of his sword. "Watch your tongue, Sir Matthew, before I cut it out!" He took a step closer. "Do you deny that one of your men killed one of mine?"

"I do not! He was defending himself. Two of your men accosted him, he engaged one of them, dispatched him with ease, then gave the other the opportunity to withdraw, which he did."

"More nonsense! No Hospitaller would withdraw from the field of battle."

"Then how did you find out what happened? It was obviously the slain man's companion that told you what transpired." He stepped closer. "Tell me something. Was he wounded?"

"What?"

"Was your second man wounded? For if he were not, then he either ran away as a coward, or was given the opportunity to withdraw honorably as Sir Damase indicated in his written report on the incident."

Bertrand took a step back, calming slightly. "Sir Damase de Sissey?"

"Yes."

He frowned. "I knew him. From Acre. He's not someone to go about murdering people." His eyes narrowed. "Why is *he* here? I thought he was in Rome."

"You know why he's here."

"I assure you I do not."

"Don't play the fool with me, sir, we both know what you've been up to. And that's why you killed him. He was about to expose you."

Bertrand shook his head. "I have no idea what you're talking about."

"You expect me to believe that? Your men murdered dozens last night, and yet you deny it?"

Bertrand's eyes widened. "We did no such thing!"

"There were witnesses!" Matthew stepped closer, aiming a finger at Bertrand's chest. "We expect the children you kidnapped to be immediately freed. If anything happens to them, the Pope will hear about it."

Bertrand went crimson, closing the gap between them. "You dare accuse my order of such horrors, then threaten me? I think it's time the Templars were taken down a peg. Your arrogance has driven you mad!"

"*My* arrogance! The Hospitallers have long been a thorn in our side, and that of the Church. It's a wonder you weren't ordered disbanded long ago."

"It is our order that will long outlast yours! Your days are numbered, Templar. All of your days!"

Bertrand spun on his heel and stormed out, his small contingent of guards rushing after him, leaving Matthew fuming. He returned to his desk and sat, reviewing the heated discussion and the Hospitaller's repeated denials.

Then the negation of his entire argument.

Your days are numbered.

It could only mean one thing.

The Hospitallers had indeed found out about René, and the fact he had broken the code.

And they intended to use that knowledge.

Sir Gotfried's Headquarters
Paris, Kingdom of France

"Vivienne! Grace!"

René rushed toward his sisters as they squealed, scrambling from their huddled embrace in the corner of the dark room and into his arms. They hugged hard for what felt like an eternity, an eternity he hoped would never end, his relief at seeing them safe overwhelming. Tears flowed freely among all three siblings while two Hospitaller knights stood watch in the hallway, a woman observing the reunion with a smile.

"Are you two well? Did they hurt you?"

Vivienne's shoulders shook as she gasped out a reply. "We thought you might be dead! Where were you? Why did you leave us alone?"

His heart broke and his chest heaved at his betrayal of them. He never should have left them, he never should have trusted they would be fine on their own. At the time, it never occurred to him that they might come to some harm. Vivienne was old enough to take care of herself and her sister, but he hadn't taken Pequin into account.

You should have left them with the neighbors.

Yet that wouldn't have worked either. Pequin, when he came searching for them, would have simply started intimidating the neighbors until one finally told him where they were hidden.

He had no choice, yet there was no way his sisters would understand.

"That's enough. Come with us."

René glanced over his shoulder at the woman, beckoning him toward the door, the guards already having stepped closer. He turned back to his sisters, wiping their cheeks dry with his thumbs. "I have to go now, but I'll be back."

"Don't leave us again!" cried Grace, both of them wrapping their arms around his neck once more. His chest ached with their wails, yet he had to put on the brave face. He forced a smile then extricated himself.

"Now, I want you both to be big girls. I'll be back soon." He stepped back toward the door and the woman intercepted his sisters as they rushed after him.

"Back to your bed. I'll bring you a snack if you stop crying."

The offer of a bribe didn't work, and the wails continued as the door closed, their little fists slamming on the door as they begged for his return. He wiped his own cheeks dry, taking deep, slow breaths as he prepared for what was to come. He hadn't seen Alain since they had been brought here, but he had heard a vicious beating delivered over at least an hour, and was certain it was the poor soul he had been captured with.

At first, he had felt little pity for the man, though as the cries for mercy continued, then the demands to God to take him so he could be with his father began, his cold heart thawed, and he realized Alain was as much a victim as he was. Alain was simple, a fool, and treated like dirt his entire life. He had fallen in with the wrong crowd, a crowd that gave him the sense of family, the sense of belonging he had been craving.

No matter how dysfunctional.

And he knew his sorrow. Alain had just lost his

father in a most horrid way, as René had. The pain was fresh, raw, and would be with him for a long time.

A very long time.

A door was opened ahead of him and he was shoved inside. Someone groaned in the corner and René gasped at the sight of a badly beaten and bruised Alain, his entire face swollen to the point his own father wouldn't recognize him, his body crumpled into a corner like a pile of discarded bones.

And if his wheezing was any indication, he might just get his wish and join his father soon.

"What have you done to him?"

He was grabbed and shoved into a chair, his hands and feet bound to it.

"He didn't answer questions." The knight stood in front of him, staring down with a lecherous smile. "Now it's your turn."

A gloved hand drove into his face, followed by another, then another. The pain was overwhelming, his nose soon broken, his mouth filling with blood as his face swelled.

Yet no questions were asked.

And the blows continued.

"What do you want from me?" he cried, and he heard his sisters scream down the hallway in response to their brother's plea.

Yet still, no questions were asked.

"P-please, I'll tell you anything!"

More blows, his torturer turning his attention to his chest and stomach, a rib cracking after a few fists landed.

"Please, just ask me a question!"

And the punches continued to rain down on him, unrelenting, without mercy, and in silence, the only sounds in his darkening world that of fist on flesh, his own cries for mercy, and the wails of his sisters in the distance.

And nothing from his interrogator.

Nothing at all.

Outside St. Mandel, Kingdom of France

"This man is no knight." Simon pointed at the body discovered moments before by Tanya's expert nose. "Look at his equipment."

Marcus agreed, kneeling beside the man. "And he's definitely not a Hospitaller." He made a quick search of the body. "And I'm not sure he killed Damase. He has no crossbow on him, nor bolts."

"So, there was a second man. Could *he* have been a Hospitaller?"

Marcus regarded his Sergeant. "That would be quite the coincidence, would it not?"

Simon shrugged. "Perhaps the Hospitaller who survived his encounter with Damase hired this man to help him."

"Perhaps, though I doubt it. He would merely have sent a message for reinforcements, then followed him." He shook his head. "No, I don't think Hospitallers had anything to do with this."

Simon was clearly disappointed. "Then what do you think happened?"

Marcus stood. "I think Damase realized he had encountered René, gave chase, and men working for Pequin intervened to protect their asset."

"But we know Hospitallers raided Pequin's place and killed everyone. And we also know Damase had an altercation with two Hospitallers, killing one of them. Are you saying that's just coincidence?"

"Yes."

Simon stared at him. "Really? Isn't that a stretch?"

Marcus chuckled. "Not at all. How many times have we had run-ins with those poor excuses for knights? A dozen? Two dozen? They usually back off once challenged, but two Hospitallers, outside of town, encountering a lone Templar of Sir Damase's age? They might get a little bolder than they should."

"So, you're saying the entire Hospitaller angle here has nothing to do with the Hospitallers in Paris."

"Exactly." Marcus pointed at the body. "Here's your proof. If it were related, they would be trying to stop Damase from uncovering the truth. They would have sent a contingent to kill him, not relied on a pathetic soul who if a mercenary, is clearly unskilled at his job, since he was not only killed, but is dressed in the rags of a peasant."

Simon nodded. "Like most of Pequin's men." He sighed. "Fine, you've convinced me. Hospitallers didn't kill Damase. Now what?"

"Now, we head back to Paris and bring Sir Matthew up to date. We can't have them thinking Hospitallers killed Damase, like the dispatch suggested. We could end up at war with them."

"But if they know about the code, might we not regardless?"

Marcus frowned. "We might, but if we're going to war, I'd like it to be for the right reasons."

Thibault Residence
Paris, Kingdom of France

"You're a brave woman to be spreading that rumor."

Simone regarded the man sitting across from her, a long-term debtor in to make his regular weekly payment.

Interest only, no progress made on the principal of the loan.

Just the way she liked it.

"It's not a rumor, it's a fact."

The man shrugged. "Well, whether it is or isn't, isn't the point now, is it? Not that I would do it, mind you, but should someone tell the Templars that you're spreading this, they might just pay you a visit."

Simone smiled slightly. "The Templars won't be long for this earth. I don't fear walking dead men."

The man shook his head. "You're braver than I am, ma'am. I would fear the walking dead if I were in your position, but then I'm a simple baker." He rose and bowed slightly. "I'll see you next week to make my payment." He headed for the door then smiled slightly. "That's assuming the walking dead haven't caught up to you!" He roared with laughter as his footfalls faded on the stairs, leaving Simone frowning in her chair, her chest tight.

The man was right.

Spreading the word so publicly was dangerous. She needed others to be doing the dirty work, otherwise it could be her neck.

"Enzo!"

The beast lumbered in. "Yes, ma'am?"

"Send for Thomas."

Enclos du Temple, Templar Fortress
Paris, Kingdom of France

"And be wary of any Hospitallers you may encounter. Trouble is brewing."

David frowned as the sergeant at the Templar fortress brought them up to date on events as they awaited Sir Matthew to become available. "Has there been any word from Sir Marcus?"

The sergeant nodded. "Yes. The last we have on him is that he was in St. Mandel, looking into the murder of Sir Damase de Sissey."

David exchanged a shocked look with Jeremy. "He's dead? How?"

"Two Hospitallers attacked Sir Damase without provocation. He killed one, but the second escaped. We believe that man then sought revenge and succeeded. But don't worry, satisfaction has been demanded. Just last night Sir Matthew met with their prior, Sir Bertrand, then sent a messenger after him with our demands."

"And they are?"

"We want the escaped coward handed over, along with whoever else was responsible for Sir Damase's subsequent murder. If they don't hand them over to stand trial, then we will take them by force."

David frowned, his heart hammering with the possible implications. "But what will the King say? Or the Pope? Shouldn't they be consulted?"

Sir Matthew entered the room and they all bowed. "No. You don't understand what's going on."

David tensed, uncertain of whether he should reveal what he knew. He decided honesty was best, and the most expedient. "We're aware of what Sir Damase was investigating."

Matthew nodded, beckoning them to follow him to his office. "Ahh, I wasn't aware. Then I will say this. The Hospitallers are involved, and should they be given a chance to act, we may lose everything."

"So, you're hoping for a confrontation."

"I am. There is no way they'll hand over their men for trial. That will force an encounter, an encounter that with our numbers, will force them to send every man they have in the area just to stand a chance."

Jeremy's eyes bulged. "Surely they can't think they'll win!"

Matthew grunted then sat behind his desk. "They might think it, but they won't. We will be victorious and vanquish any in these lands, putting an end to the fake Letters of Credit, allowing us to deny it all as Hospitaller propaganda, and move on."

David stared at his shoes, uncomfortable with pointing out a flaw in the plan. "But what of those who know?"

Matthew shrugged. "Beyond the Hospitallers, only peasants seem to know, and who would believe them?"

Thomas murmured, "I would."

Matthew smiled. "Ahh, Master Thomas Durant. And just how are you involved in this?"

Thomas paled. "I, umm, know the man behind this."

"You know René Courvat?"

"Yes, sir."

"Then perhaps *you* three can find him. He and his sisters are missing. We know the Hospitallers have his sisters, though they deny it, of course, but René was last seen in St. Mandel. The fact Sir Damase was giving chase suggests that either René is the one who murdered him—"

"Not a chance!" interrupted Thomas. "He's not the sort!"

"—or he escaped when the Hospitallers murdered Damase, and perhaps is heading back to Paris. Find him for me. He is the key to putting an end to this."

David bowed. "Yes, sir, we'll do our best."

Matthew dismissed them and the three of them bowed, returning to the courtyard where they mounted freshly provisioned horses. David turned to Thomas.

"Where should we start?"

"René's house, I suppose."

"How far is it from here?"

"Perhaps a quarter-hour ride. Not far."

David urged his horse forward. "Then let's make all haste. I hadn't planned on receiving orders from Sir Matthew. I would have preferred to head for St. Mandel and find Sir Marcus."

Jeremy grunted. "We could always disobey. We're not exactly full members of the Order anymore."

David gave him the eye. "*I* will be a full member of the Order until the day I die, even if I shovel shit and plant crops rather than fight the heathen Saracens."

Jeremy stared at him. "You know I was just joking."

David grinned. "I know, but where's the fun in that." He urged his horse faster. "If we're lucky, perhaps we can accomplish both tasks today."

"Shoveling shit *and* planting crops?"

David laughed as they rode through the fortress gates, his chest aching at the sight of so many Templar brothers.

I do miss this.

En Route to Paris, Kingdom of France

"This can't be good."

Marcus frowned at the sight ahead of them. Six Hospitallers on horseback, riding three abreast to make certain no one could pass unchallenged. "Keep your sword sheathed until we see what they want."

"Isn't it obvious?"

"They could simply be passing through."

"Are you Sir Marcus de Rancourt?" asked the commander, pulling out ahead as he came to a stop, the remaining men spreading across the road.

"You were saying?" muttered Simon.

Marcus put his hand on the hilt of his sword. "I am."

"You had to tell them."

The commander sneered. "Then prepare to defend yourself!"

Six swords unsheathed and Marcus cursed, drawing his own as he quickly assessed the situation. They were outnumbered three to one, though that only mattered if the six they faced were experienced in battle, and with Hospitallers, it was a definite possibility.

Tanya surged forward, barking and snarling, the mastiff no match in size for the horses, but big enough and fierce enough to have two of them rearing on their hind legs in panic.

"Good girl!" smiled Marcus as he charged, the brief distraction reducing the immediate threat to four as the other two riders struggled to regain control of their mounts. Marcus headed for the two on the right, which included the commander, angling his attack so only one could be a threat on his first pass, the other blocked by his partner.

The commander swung his sword and Marcus leaned out of the way, keeping his sword unengaged, then righted himself, thrusting forward and catching the unsuspecting second man in the chest, piercing his armor enough to weaken his arm, his sword clattering to the ground. Marcus continued forward, tossing his sword into his other hand then shoving the blade under the ribcage of one of the struggling riders, Tanya still nipping at the horse's neck.

He turned around to see Simon had dispatched two of his own and was now engaged in an epic struggle with the commander and one other, a string of curses and clever insults erupting from his sergeant's mouth as he held his own.

Marcus urged his well-trained beast back into the fray and pointed at the commander. "Tanya, get him!"

Tanya turned, charging the man from behind and leaped through the air, latching onto his back, causing him to cry out in terror as her snarling fangs snapped at his head. Marcus pierced the wounded Hospitaller's chest, ending his suffering, as Simon dispatched his last man, leaving only the commander.

"Tanya, stop!"

She immediately broke away, rushing to his side, panting, her tail wagging as the defeated knight, now all alone, gripped his neck, the blood flowing freely, his time on this earth clearly limited.

Marcus approached him, his sword held in front of him. "Do you yield?"

The man glared at him defiantly. "I will never yield."

"Then you will die."

The man drew his dagger, dropping his sword. "Not by your hand, Templar!" He plunged the tip into his heart and gasped, collapsing forward on his horse, the startled animal bolting as its master took his last breaths lying on its back.

"Should I go get him?"

Marcus shook his head. "He's already dead." He surveyed the situation, shaking his head at the sight of five dead Hospitallers, their horses skittish though calming, one bloodied sergeant, and one happy mastiff. "This was unnecessary."

"Agreed. They should have known to send a dozen."

Marcus chuckled. "They're getting bolder. First Sir Damase, now this. I think they sense our imminent demise."

Simon regarded him. "You mean with word of the broken code spreading?"

"Exactly. It's hard to fear an enemy that may well be brought to its knees in days."

Simon grunted. "Well, these six will certainly fear us."

"They're dead. I'm not sure there's much fear left in them."

Simon laughed. "You're right, of course, but it will certainly give their brothers second thoughts." He relaxed in his saddle. "Speaking of second thoughts, are you still convinced they had nothing to do with Damase's murder?"

"Yes. These men were sent to kill *me* specifically, not

just any Templar."

"But why you?"

"They must know we are investigating this situation, and are trying to stop us."

Simon's eyes narrowed. "But how would they know?"

Marcus shook his head. "I don't know. Only Matthew knew we were assisting Damase, and where we were."

"Alain's father?"

"No, he only knew we were looking for him and that we had headed east out of the city, but not to where. These men were on the only road that leads from St. Mandel to Paris. They knew the path we'd be taking."

Simon frowned. "So, there's a spy somewhere."

"I'm afraid you might be right. And whoever it is, seems to have direct access to Matthew himself." Marcus sheathed his sword. "We need to report this immediately. Our brothers could be in danger."

"Should we head back to St. Mandel and report it, or continue to Paris?"

"Paris. We'll report it in person faster than any messenger could should we backtrack." He urged his horse forward. "Let's go!"

Unknown Location
Paris, Kingdom of France

"Wh-where am I?"

René felt hands on him as several people carried him inside a building. He had been taken by carriage from where, he did not know, his journey marked by blackouts no doubt brought on by the vicious beating he had received.

Where not a single question was asked.

He had been tossed onto the street moments before and words were exchanged, words he either couldn't understand or couldn't hear, his ears pounding with the rushing of blood. His entire body was in agony, even more so now that he was manhandled with no regard as to what might be broken.

Then bliss.

He was on something soft, then was lifted into the air, the tiny sliver he could see through one eye telling him he was being carried on a stretcher deeper into the building, men and women hurrying about tending to the ill and infirm.

He was in a hospital.

"My sisters. Where are my sisters?"

"Just keep still. You've been badly beaten."

He pushed up on his elbows but cried out as an unbelievable pain erupted from his shoulder.

"Just stay down. Your shoulder is dislocated."

"My sisters," he whispered. "Somebody save my sisters."

They came to a stop and the light was blocked as someone leaned over him. Fingers gently probed his face then body, a man's voice listing off what he found, including several broken bones and cracked ribs.

But none of that mattered.

He reached out and grabbed the man, ignoring his pain.

"What is it, son?"

"My sisters. You must save them."

"Who has them?"

"The Hospitallers. They did this."

"What? But that's impossible."

He shook his head slightly. "No, sir, it's not. They did this. They have my sisters."

"But, son, it can't be true."

"It is!"

"But you don't understand. *We're* Hospitallers."

René forced his eyes opened and gasped at the sight. All around him were men and women, hard at work, all with black shirts with white crosses.

The markings of the Order of Hospitallers.

He collapsed, shaking his head, tears pouring from his eyes. "What kind of sick, twisted people are you?"

Enclos du Temple, Templar Fortress
Paris, Kingdom of France

"Has there been any word?"

The sergeant shook his head at Sir Matthew's question. "None as of yet, sir."

Matthew cursed, his head shaking. He surveyed the scores of knights gathered in the courtyard of the fortress, their squires readying them and their horses for war. It was to be a show of force designed to overwhelm any possible idea of resistance by the dishonorable Hospitallers.

Justice would be won tonight, and he suspected not a drop of blood would be shed if those cowards held true to form.

"Then we march." He beckoned a messenger over. "Send a dispatch to all outposts in the area to instruct our people to not travel alone, and to be wary of any Hospitallers. There will be revenge attacks, I'm certain."

"Yes, sir." The messenger rushed inside to fulfill his orders, and Matthew turned to face the large contingent, and they fell silent.

"Today, we march on the Hospitaller fortress for justice! These dishonorable Hospitallers murdered one of our own, Sir Damase de Sissey, and his death will not go unpunished. These pathetic excuses for knights must be put in their place. They will rue the day they crossed our order." He clenched a fist, shoving it in the air. "Mark my words, before this day is out, we will put an end to their insolence, and find justice for Sir

Damase!"

Fists and swords were raised as those gathered, knight and squire, priest and stable boy, roared their approval, and a surge of pride and bravado rushed through him. With men such as these, how could they possibly lose? The very sight of so many knights on horseback, gathered in one place, had his heart aching for the days when he had served in the Holy Land, where a call to arms as he had issued would have meant a thousand knights alone.

But the number gathered here today would be more than enough.

For the Hospitallers were new in this area, and few in number, their entire purpose here the establishment of a hospital. At least that was their story. He suspected, as did others among the leadership of the Order, that they were here to garner favor with King Philip, a man who wasn't a fan of the Templars, likely because he owed a princely sum to the Order.

He was about to give the command to march when a peasant rushed the gates, waving something in his hand. Four guards quickly grabbed him before he could gain entry, two of them bringing him over several moments later.

"He demands to see someone in charge, sir."

Matthew eyed the man from atop his horse. He was filthy, clearly a beggar of sorts, and not the type to normally have business with the Order. "What is it you want?"

The man waved a paper gripped in his hand. "I have a message for you."

"From whom?"

"I-I don't know. He paid me ten deniers to deliver

it to you."

Matthew reached down and plucked the page from the man's fingers, examining it. It was folded as a message normally was, though there was no seal or other identifying marks.

But it was addressed to him.

He unfolded it and read the message, rage filling him at the words.

The Hospitallers have René Courvat at their hospital.

He stared down at the man, his eyes boring into him. "Who gave this to you?"

"I swear, I don't know."

"What did he look like?"

He shrugged. "Like any man, though of higher station than I."

"A knight?"

"Perhaps."

"Did he have any markings. A tunic with his order's emblem?"

The man shook his head. "I-I don't think so, but my eyes aren't very good anymore."

Matthew's jaw squared as he turned to his men. "This message says the Hospitallers have the man we seek. The bastards have lied to us!" He drew his sword, raising it high in the air. "To their hospital, where we shall reveal the full extent of their treachery!"

Outside the Courvat Residence
Paris, Kingdom of France

"Yes, I saw him. He was here last night."

Thomas watched as David held his horse by the reins, having dismounted so as not to intimidate the neighbors of René Courvat. "Where'd he go?"

"I don't know, but he took off when he heard some of Pequin's men had taken his sisters. But he got his."

Jeremy eyed him. "What do you mean?"

"Pequin's dead. So are all his men."

Thomas' eyes bulged, his stomach churning. "What happened?"

"They were slaughtered. By Hospitallers, no less! Can you believe it?"

David shook his head. "No, I can't."

"It's true. Pequin himself told that Templar Knight that was here yesterday."

"Sir Marcus de Rancourt?"

The man shrugged. "How should I know?"

David gave up. "Where is this place?"

The man pointed farther down the street. "Just around the corner. Can't miss it."

"Thank you for your help."

They mounted their horses and headed for the tavern, Thomas leading the way. "It's called the Shrieking Owl. It's Pequin's headquarters. He—"

His jaw dropped at the sight ahead. People were milling about, and none of the nightlife that should have already begun was in sight. A priest and a murmur of nuns were praying in front, and several candles that appeared to be in remembrance of some tragedy were lit and placed on the windowsills of the darkened establishment.

David rode up to the priest and dismounted. "I'm sorry to interrupt, Father, but can you tell me what's happened here?"

The priest regarded him for a moment, and upon noticing his brown tunic with red cross, softened his expression. "I'm afraid I cannot tell you much." He pointed at a man across the street, regaling a group with a story that appeared to have them hanging on every word. "I suggest you speak with him. He seems to know more than most."

David bowed. "Thank you, Father."

They walked their horses across the street, the crowd parting for the two Templar squires and Thomas' insignificant self. "I understand you can tell us what happened here."

"Aye, I can," replied the man who hopped off his perch, revealing himself to be all of four feet tall, if that. "What would you like to know?"

"Everything." David smiled. "If you don't mind."

The little man shrugged. "Sure, why not. It was Hospitallers. They came in, killed everyone including Pequin, then left."

"How can you be sure it was Hospitallers?"

"I saw them myself."

David's eyebrows shot up. "You were there?"

The man nodded. "Yes. I was one of the few to survive."

Jeremy glanced over his shoulder at the tavern.

"How did you manage it?"

"I hid behind the bar."

David indicated the man's stature. "Then how did you, umm, see them?"

The man flushed, shifting from one foot to the other. "Well, I didn't actually see them, but I heard Pequin talking to one of them, and he said something like, 'I thought you Hospitallers were supposed to be men of honor,' and the other said something I couldn't quite understand."

"Why not?"

"He had an accent. It was quite thick."

"So, he wasn't French?"

"No, definitely not."

"English? German? Spanish?"

He threw up his hands. "How should I know? I just know he wasn't French. Does it matter? Even you Templars aren't all French, are you?"

David smiled slightly. "No, nor are Hospitallers." He folded his arms, not entirely convinced of the man's story. "So, you didn't see them? Even when they came in?"

"Well, I did, I guess, for a few moments, but they rushed in with their swords drawn, and I just jumped over the bar and tucked into one of the drawers."

"*You* jumped over the bar?"

The man scowled. "I was sitting on the bar, if you must know, and I rolled off and fell behind it. Happy? Happy that you've made the dwarf embarrass himself with the truth? Happy that you've shamed a man cursed by God since birth?"

David's cheeks flushed with embarrassment and he

shook his head. "No, I meant no offense. It's just that it's critically important we know all the facts, and that they're accurate. The implications of Hospitallers being involved is significant, as I'm sure you can guess."

"I suppose."

David sighed, gesturing at the man. "If you survived because you were able to hide in a drawer, then perhaps God blessed you after all."

"What do you mean?"

"Well, consider if you were of average height. You'd be dead now like the others."

The man thought for a moment then his eyes shot wide and he grinned. "I guess I never thought of it like that. You're right!"

David smiled, pleased the uncomfortable situation was resolved. "Was René Courvat in here yesterday or today?"

Someone else answered from the crowd. "He was here last night, looking for his sisters."

"His sisters?

"Yes, Pequin took them as, shall we say, collateral, but those Hospitallers ended up taking them."

David frowned. "Do you know where René is now?"

The man shrugged. "No idea, but the priest told him about some Templars like you that might be able to help. They were looking for Alain."

"Templars? Was one named Sir Marcus?"

"No idea."

Jeremy stepped forward. "Did they have a dog with them?"

The man's eyes widened, and several in the crowd

nodded. "Yes! A huge beast!"

Jeremy grinned at David. "That's them."

David agreed. "Do you know where René went?"

"I think he went looking for Alain in order to find your friends."

"Who's he?"

"One of Pequin's men. A moron, but loyal. Watch out for him. He's dangerous when confused."

"Where might we find him?"

"Try his father's. That's where I'd go. Do you need a guide?"

David beckoned Thomas forward. "This young man is local."

A hush went over the crowd and Thomas cringed, those gathered obviously recognizing him as someone who worked for Simone. And that included the man they were speaking to.

"Master Durant, I didn't recognize you."

Thomas forced a smile. "Sir."

"Umm, do you know the blacksmith about a mile from here?"

"I do."

"Well, that's Alain's father."

David bowed slightly. "Thank you for your help." He turned to the survivor. "And thank you, sir."

The man bowed with a flourish. "Always happy to help the Templars. Just send a little money this way soon."

The crowd roared with laughter, leaving them all curious as they mounted their horses and left the area behind them.

"What do you think that was about?" asked Jeremy.

David frowned. "I'm not sure, but I sure hope it doesn't have to do with the code being broken." He sighed. "Everyone back there certainly seems convinced Hospitallers are behind this."

Jeremy nodded. "Agreed." He motioned at the road ahead of them. "I have a feeling we're going to be running all around Paris futilely trying to find this René guy. If he was looking for Sir Marcus and found him, then our search is pointless. And if he didn't find him, wouldn't he seek out our help at the fortress?"

"I doubt it since he's our code breaker. Let's go to this blacksmith and see if René made it there. If the trail goes cold, we'll report back to the fortress to see if there have been any updates on Sir Marcus or René."

They all turned in their saddles at the sound of someone galloping behind them, calling for the crowd they had just left behind to make way. Thomas relaxed as he spotted the Templar tunic of one of their messengers.

Then nearly soiled himself at what came out of his mouth.

"One of the people back there said I could find Master Thomas Durant in your company." His eyes fell on Thomas. "Are you he?"

Thomas trembled. "I am."

"Then you must come with me at once."

David edged his horse forward. "What is this about?"

The messenger shook his head. "I'm not privy to that information, but if you are Squires David and Jeremy, then you are to come as well, by order of Sir Matthew Norris."

David's eyes widened as he exchanged a concerned

glance with Jeremy. "Then lead on and make haste!"

The messenger turned around and charged off, the two squires following without hesitation, leaving Thomas behind, still shaking in his saddle, wondering what the Templar commander for the entire Kingdom of France could possibly want with him.

David turned in his saddle. "Master Thomas! Let's go!"

Thomas reluctantly urged his steed forward, slowly gaining speed as he willed himself toward what, he did not know.

He just knew it couldn't be good.

St. John's Hospital
Paris, Kingdom of France

Matthew strode through the main entrance of the newly established hospital, his men already inside, overwhelming the few guards on duty, any escape blocked by a barrier of beast and man surrounding the establishment.

As he continued inside unchallenged, the shouts on the main floor now few, and those above fading, he smiled at the fear and anger in the eyes of those they now subdued. For it was a humiliating defeat.

No battle had taken place here today.

Beyond a few injuries, there was nothing.

And as there was no possibility of defeat, the victory was unsatisfactory.

That will come later.

"Who's in charge here?"

A man with at least somewhat of a regal bearing stepped forward. "I am. What is the meaning of this incursion? We are a place of healing, not war!"

Matthew ignored him. "I am Sir Matthew Norris. We are seeking a man named René Courvat. Where is he?"

"You are holding my people at knifepoint. We have people here who are sick and dying. They must be attended to! How dare you put their lives at risk!"

Matthew stepped closer to the man, gripping the hilt of his sword. "Then you should be answering my questions quickly, rather than delaying."

The man glared at him then cursed. "What was the name again?"

"René Courvat."

The man stepped over to a desk, picking up several sheets of paper, quickly flipping through them. "We have no one here by that name."

Matthew held his tongue, the temptation to run the liar through overwhelming. "And how can you be so certain?"

The man held up the pages. "This is a list of everyone here."

Matthew took the pages and quickly scanned them, not finding their target's name. "You have some with just an X."

"Those are the ones whose names we don't know."

"Why?"

"They either can't speak or are unconscious."

Matthew smiled slightly, hope still remaining. "Show us them."

"Very well." The Hospitaller led Matthew through the hospital, the level of suffering here heartbreaking, forcing even his angry heart to soften at the sight.

He sighed. "Tell your people they can go back to work." He held up a finger. "But if they try anything, I'll slit their throats personally."

The man nodded. "Thank you." He issued the orders as Matthew's sergeant spread the word to their men, then resumed visiting the beds of those whose names were merely an X on a page. By the end of the tour, Matthew had identified only three that generally matched the description they had for René from Damase's message, all on the second floor in an area reserved for the worst cases.

"I need the names of these three men."

"But they're all unconscious."

"Wake them."

"How? Would you have me slap them until they awaken? All three of these men are unconscious because they have suffered head trauma. This one was kicked in the head by the horse of a nobleman. This one was found beaten in an alleyway, and this one was dropped off here just hours ago, badly beaten, babbling incoherently before mercifully passing out."

Matthew paused, staring at the third man. "What was he saying?"

"I'm not sure, something about his sisters."

A smile spread on Matthew's face as he turned to his sergeant. "This is him. Has Master Thomas arrived yet?"

"No, sir."

"I want him found! He's the only one who can positively identify this man. Before I order every Hospitaller in this city arrested, I want my proof confirmed!"

Enclos du Temple, Templar Fortress
Paris, Kingdom of France

Marcus' eyes narrowed as they passed through the main gates of the Templar fortress, finding few of the usually abundant knights. They proceeded to check in at the main entrance, the sergeant on duty appearing on edge.

"What's going on, sergeant?"

The man closed his eyes for a moment then sighed. He opened them, his eyebrows shooting up as he recognized them. "Sir Marcus! Thank the good Lord you are well. We weren't sure what had happened to you."

"I'm fine as well," muttered Simon.

"Of course, of course. It's just that so much has happened since you left."

"I need to report an attack."

The man's eyebrows rose. "An attack? What sort of attack?"

"Six Hospitallers on horseback attacked us on our way here, just outside of the city."

"And you're uninjured?"

Simon grunted. "Of course, they were Hospitallers, and there were only six of them."

The man smiled broadly. "Ahh, to see battle again." He patted his leg, revealing a stump. "Alas, it is not to be." He assessed them quickly. "And what should the report say became of the Hospitallers?"

Simon sneered. "They were dispatched with no mercy."

Marcus chuckled. "Just say we were victorious, uninjured, and that the six Hospitallers are now being judged by the good Lord."

"I'm pleased to hear it." He scribbled down some notes then returned his attention to the new arrivals. "I'm afraid that there is a situation, and it interestingly involves the Hospitallers."

Marcus tensed. "Yes?"

"Sir Matthew has asked me to brief you should you return. We have found proof of the Hospitallers' treachery. They denied involvement in the matter Sir Damase was investigating—I'm sorry, I'm not privy to the details, however Sir Matthew assured me you were."

"We are."

"Very well. They apparently denied any involvement, including knowing the whereabouts of Mr. René Courvat. We received an anonymous tip that René was being held at their new hospital. Sir Matthew left about an hour ago to take the hospital by force and acquire the evidence needed to prove the Hospitaller involvement in whatever matter it is you are investigating."

Marcus exchanged an excited glance with Simon at the news. "Any instructions?"

"You are to join him immediately."

Marcus smiled, sensing action in their future. "Very well. We'll need fresh horses and a guide."

The sergeant turned to a stable boy standing nearby and snapped his fingers. "You heard him. Two fresh horses plus one for me."

"Yes, sir!" The boy hopped in place then rushed off to execute his orders.

The sergeant stood, grabbing a crutch that lay beside

him. "If you don't mind, I'll be your guide, sir."

Marcus didn't bother challenging the man's ability. If a man of honor felt he was capable, then who was he to question it. "Very well." He stared after the boy, scratching his beard as he thought of the events of the past couple of days. "Was he here the entire time?"

The sergeant shrugged. "I'm not sure. I never pay him any mind until I need him, and he seems to always be there when I do."

Marcus turned to Simon. "I'm certain he was the same one we noticed in the room when Matthew gave us our initial briefing."

Simon shrugged. "Dunno. You know me and kids. I can barely tell Jacques and Angeline apart."

"Is it important?" asked the sergeant.

Marcus nodded. "We have reason to believe there's a spy in our midst."

"Impossible!"

"Is it? While I doubt any of our sworn members are involved, we know little of these boys that serve us. Any one of them could easily have their loyalty purchased."

"You suspect this boy in particular?"

Marcus frowned, his gut telling him something untoward was happening. "I do, though I have no proof. Do you have a boy you can trust?"

"I do."

"Then fetch him for me at once."

St. John's Hospital
Paris, Kingdom of France

"Is that him?"

Thomas stared at the bloody pulp of a man, horrified that any human could do such a thing to another, and it made him wonder if this was what Enzo did to those he identified as late on their payments.

It made him sick.

"I-I can't be sure. I think so, but, well…"

Matthew placed a hand on his shoulder. "I know it's a gruesome sight, boy, but if any good is going to come from this man's suffering, it depends on you being sure. I can't go to war on 'I think so.'"

The beaten man's eyes fluttered open, at least as far as they could, and his hand reached for Thomas. "Thomas! What happened?"

Thomas recognized the voice and stepped closer, taking the man's hand. "You were beaten and left here. I'm so sorry."

"My sisters. They have my sisters." He pulled Thomas closer. "You must save them!"

"Who has them?"

René let go of his hand then pointed at the Hospitaller tunic of the man in charge. "They do!" He collapsed, unconscious again, but the few words he had spoken were damning.

And convincing.

Matthew slapped his hands together. "That's all the proof I need. Gather them all together and place them under guard!"

"Absolutely not!" protested the Hospitaller. "We have patients to tend to!"

Matthew glared at him for a moment then relaxed slightly. "How many do you need?"

"All of us!"

Matthew shook his head. "Out of the question." He took in the activity that continued around them, coming to a decision. "You can have all your nuns and six doctors. None armed. The rest will be held until this is all sorted."

"But you're killing these people!"

Matthew stepped closer. "My good sir, I would be worried more about my own life at this moment, than theirs. The Pope has granted us authority in this matter, and justice will be done before this day is through."

The Hospitaller squared his shoulders, glaring at Matthew. "I will die with my honor intact, sir, though I can't say the same for you, should you fall during your attempt to bring us down."

Matthew sneered. "The Hospitallers are no match for us."

"Perhaps not, which is why I would suggest to you that we would do nothing to act against you, especially here in Paris, where our numbers are few compared to yours." He inched closer, lowering his voice slightly. "But remember this, Templar. Even in the most one-sided of battles, some of the victors die. You may be one of them, and you will answer for what you have done here today." He waved his hand at those suffering around them. "The blood of these innocents is on your hands."

Matthew regarded him for a moment. "Very well."

He turned to his sergeant. "Remove all their weapons from the premises then withdraw. Guard the perimeter. No one goes in or out." He turned back to the Hospitaller. "No one."

The man bowed deeply. "Thank you, Sir Matthew."

"Don't thank me yet, sir. You still may not live the night."

Leaving the Enclos du Temple, Templar Fortress
Paris, Kingdom of France

Quentin's heart bounded with excitement at his assignment. He had been an orphan as long as he could remember, his uncle dropping him off at the entrance to the Templar fortress as soon as he could walk. The monks had taken him in, raised him, and kept him warm, dry, and well fed. And in exchange, he cleaned the stables and did other odd jobs, in the hopes of one day becoming a squire, and perhaps even a sergeant.

That would be the dream!

And an assignment like this, should he succeed, could be his ticket to a bright future.

When asked to keep an eye on Henri, one of his fellow stable boys, he had been honored.

And terrified.

But mostly honored.

Yet he had to be careful about it, for simply staring at him would make him suspicious.

He thought he had been clever about it, simply staying in the same general vicinity with a broom, for there was always something to sweep.

Then when Henri had left without asking, he had followed, using anything he could find to keep out of sight. And when Henri finally arrived at his destination, he stood in the middle of the street slack-jawed, his eyes bulging at the implications.

He's a traitor!

He bolted for the fortress then froze in his tracks.

The knight that had assigned him the task had left with a sergeant to join the battle at the hospital, which was where Sir Matthew was as well.

Everyone who needed to know what he now did was there.

And he knew where it was.

Sir Gotfried's Headquarters
Paris, Kingdom of France

"The Templars have just attacked St. John's Hospital."

Gotfried smiled at Konrad's news. "Exactly as planned." He leaned forward. "Please tell me they shed blood."

Konrad nodded. "Our man says they did, though it appears to be minimal."

Gotfried frowned. "Unfortunate. I hate to see the blood of innocents shed needlessly, though the ends sometimes justify the means." He stared at the flag of his order on the wall in front of him, its crisp black and white always an inspiration, especially when seen in a public show of force. And though they were but a small contingent here in Paris, when the Templars were brought to their knees, it would be his order that would fill the void left behind, and its rise to prominence, and dominance, would be complete.

There was a knock at the door and Konrad stepped over to open it, revealing their filthy little spy, Henri. Gotfried beckoned him inside.

"What have you to report?"

The boy gasped out his first few sentences, obviously having sprinted here the entire way. "Sir Marcus arrived at the fortress less than an hour ago."

Gotfried cursed, shaking his head at Konrad. "Six men couldn't handle two?"

"He said they were all killed," gasped Henri.

Konrad frowned. "Well, I guess we know why they

didn't report back."

"Who did he say attacked them?" asked Gotfried.

"Hospitallers."

Gotfried grunted. "At least they followed *those* orders. Where is he now?"

"Fresh horses were provided, and he and his sergeant, along with a guide, are heading to the hospital to join Sir Matthew."

"Is that all?"

Henri nodded.

"Good work, boy. Now get back before you're missed."

"Yes, sir." Henri disappeared and Gotfried leaned back.

"The plan is going perfectly, though it would have been better if Sir Marcus had been removed."

"What should we do now?"

"Nothing. The Templars will have confirmed René's identity by now, will know they were lied to, and will be marching on the Hospitaller fortress as we speak." A smile crept from the sides of his mouth. "Before this night ends, we will be the most powerful order in this and any kingdom."

St. John's Hospital
Paris, Kingdom of France

"I think we're too late."

Marcus had to agree with Simon's assessment. While the hospital was surrounded by Templar knights and sergeants, there were too few to be the entirety of the impressive force their guide had indicated should be here. He hailed one of the knights.

"We seek Sir Matthew. Is he here?"

The man advanced. "Sorry, he and the bulk of our men have already left."

Marcus frowned. "Where did they go?"

"To put an end to this Hospitaller treachery once and for all."

"And where do they intend to do that?"

"At their fortress, of course."

Marcus cursed his lack of knowledge of the area. "Where is that?"

Their guide intervened. "I know where it is. I'll take you."

"How far is it?"

"About half an hour from here if we keep a good pace."

Marcus thanked the knight then turned his horse around when a young boy came racing around the corner, shouting at the top of his lungs.

"He's a traitor! He's a traitor!"

Their guide flagged the boy down, and Marcus recognized him as the stable boy the sergeant had said could be trusted to watch their suspected spy. He stared down at the boy, his chest heaving, his hands on his knees as he caught his breath.

"Tell me, boy, why do you think he's a traitor?"

"I followed him like you asked. I saw where he went. You're right! He's a traitor!"

Marcus' eyes narrowed. If the Hospitaller fortress was half an hour from here on horseback, then where did this boy just come from on foot?

Hospitaller Fortress
Paris, Kingdom of France

David's breath caught in his throat at the sight. The Hospitaller fortress, newly established in Paris, and frankly not much of a fortification in his mind, was surrounded by Templars on horseback, torches in hand, with orders to light the place afire should Matthew give the command.

It brought back so many memories of the old days in the Holy Land, it almost had him weeping. These were his brothers, doing their duty for the Order, the Pope, the Church, and their Lord, all as one well-trained unit, no one going rogue, no one throwing their torch in anger, all simply sitting atop their horses, torches in hand, calmly waiting for the order to execute, or to stand down.

He glanced at Jeremy and smiled, his friend's eyes glistening, his chest heaving at the sight, and he knew his fellow squire missed what they had left behind. It was a constant struggle on the farm, with both having expressed their concerns, both battling the desire to leave and rejoin the brotherhood they had sworn allegiance to so long ago.

Yet they didn't. David loved his master and would never betray him. Sir Marcus had done the honorable thing and remained at the farm to raise his niece and nephew, and the rest of them had vowed to stand by his side.

They were family.

Just as these men, gathered here tonight, encircling

the Hospitaller fortification as one, were as well.

He smiled, drawing a deep breath, then turned to Jeremy. "It's a sight to behold."

"It is that," agreed his friend. "It's been so long since I've seen so many of our brothers prepared for battle, I'd almost forgotten what it looked like."

David eyed the ramparts as they approached, Matthew instructing David, Jeremy, and Thomas to remain by his side. They came to a halt about thirty paces from the front gate, its iron bars closed, torches intermittently lighting the manned positions along the walls, revealing few defenders.

Matthew shook his head at the sight. "It would appear they are either woefully undermanned, or we caught them completely off guard. They haven't had time to call for reinforcements."

That seemed odd to David. If the Hospitallers were so hellbent on destroying the Templars, wouldn't they have recalled all their men from the surrounding area? Why would they leave themselves so inadequately defended?

He held his tongue, deciding his station didn't merit questioning the situation.

Apparently, Jeremy didn't agree. "If they're doing what we think they're doing, why didn't they expect us to come here?"

Matthew turned in his saddle. "What do you mean, squire?"

Jeremy gulped at the mention of his rank. "Umm, nothing, sir. Sorry."

Matthew eyed him for a moment, then indicated for his men to hold their position, advancing several paces toward the gate. "I am Sir Matthew Norris of the

Knights Templar. I demand you immediately send out those responsible for the murder of our knight, Sir Damase de Sissey, to answer for their crimes!"

David noted Matthew didn't mention the breaking of the Templar code, probably a wise decision. To broadcast that piece of information to all the Hospitallers behind the walls, and all the Templars gathered, would mean the secret would spread like wildfire among the ranks.

The gates creaked open and the leader of the Hospitallers, along with four men carrying torches, all on horseback, rode out to confront the Templar force. The leader's expression was grim, though there was no hint of fear on his face.

Matthew bowed his head slightly. "Sir Bertrand."

The man returned the gesture. "Sir Matthew. What is the meaning of this?"

"You know very well, Sir Bertrand. We demand justice, and an end to your nefarious activities."

Bertrand shook his head. "Again with this nonsense. Nefarious activities? You sound like a raving lunatic." He drew a breath, calming himself. "Sir, if you do not withdraw, there will be no turning back. Once blood is shed, both our orders will be destroyed."

Matthew chuckled. "You think you can be victorious here today?"

"Of course not, we don't have the numbers. Here. But in the Holy Land? We do. But none of that will matter. The Pope will disband both our orders should this long-simmering conflict of ours escalate."

Matthew spat. "The Pope knows of your treachery, and gave Sir Damase, whom you murdered, full authority in the matter, beyond that of Kings. That authority now falls to me."

"Impossible! Damase was murdered yesterday, according to you. Even your famous Templar messenger network couldn't get word to Rome and back in that time." Bertrand jabbed a finger at Matthew. "You lie! Why would the Pope grant Damase authority to investigate his own murder, you fool?"

Matthew's chest expanded and his hand went to the hilt of his sword. "You know very well that's not what he was here for! Sir Damase was here to investigate the forgeries that you had Mr. René Courvat create for you!"

Bertrand's eyes widened and in David's inexpert opinion, he appeared genuinely surprised. "Forgeries? What forgeries? What the devil are you talking about?"

Matthew's sword revealed a hint of its blade. "You dare deny it when we found the forger in your own custody?"

"Who?"

"René Courvat, of course!"

"You keep saying that name, but I've never heard of him! You make no sense, Templar!" He jabbed a finger at Matthew. "We are prepared to fight, and you will pay dearly to breach these walls. But know this! Should we be defeated here tonight, my messengers have already gone out with the truth. The King, the Pope, and our order will know what you have done here, and that we are innocent. The Templars will be brought to justice and disavowed by the Church before this is done."

Matthew edged closer. "And the Hospitallers will be vanquished before that can happen."

Bertrand shook his head. "You would destroy your own order to defeat us? Why? What is it that is so important that you would risk everything? What are these forgeries? Why are they so important?" Suddenly his eyes went wide. "Oh my God! Someone has broken your code!"

Sir Gotfried's Headquarters
Paris, Kingdom of France

"There!"

Marcus looked where the boy was pointing and his heart slammed at the sight. It couldn't be. "Are you sure, boy?"

"Yes. He went in there. I saw him."

Simon's head was shaking at what stood before them.

An impossible sight.

With incredible implications.

For the flag that waved proudly across the street was not that of the Hospitallers, but that of the Teutonic Order.

Simon turned to Marcus. "What does this mean?"

Marcus shook his head. "I don't know. It makes no sense."

"Could they be working together?"

Marcus' head slowly bobbed at the suggestion. It was possible, though unlikely. The Teutons got along with the Hospitallers about as well as either order did with the Templars. It was an age-old rivalry between the three orders that would never be settled.

And as he stared at the flag, its black cross contrasting sharply with its white background, something occurred to him, and he finally realized exactly what was going on.

"We need to stop Sir Matthew before it's too late!"

Hospitaller Fortress
Paris, Kingdom of France

Thomas flinched as the iron gates slammed shut, the discussion done, their enemy unwilling to admit to their crimes, or hand over those who had murdered Damase. This was about to get ugly, yet it made no sense to him.

Why would the Hospitallers risk all-out destruction rather than hand over one or two men responsible for murdering Damase? They could easily claim they had gone rogue and committed the murder without permission.

But more was going on here from the Templar perspective. He understood why the code was so precious, and that the cracking of it could destroy the entire order by undermining the trust placed in it, and destroying the financial network that allowed it to exist in such great numbers, spread across the entirety of Europe. But these Hospitallers continued to deny their involvement, and were willing to die while maintaining their innocence.

Though if they were guilty, perhaps they were holding out hope they might survive the siege long enough for reinforcements to arrive, perhaps even from the King, no friend to the Templars. Yet their leader had appeared taken aback when he realized what was going on, though his continued denials were ignored. In fact, Matthew had said nothing, as if he couldn't bring himself to admit the code had been broken.

But if the Hospitallers didn't know, then didn't it

mean they weren't involved?

"Clear the way!"

He spun in his saddle, recognizing the voice at once, and breathed a sigh of relief at the sight of what he hoped were cooler heads arriving.

Marcus charged between the marshaled forces, his empty hands held up. He slowed as he approached the gate then came to a halt. He stood high in his saddle, searching the crowd for Matthew as he spoke. "Please, lower your weapons! We have all been played for fools!"

Matthew rode forward, Marcus sitting back in his saddle once he spotted him. "Sir Marcus, explain yourself!"

The man was angry, and it was clear Marcus had arrived just in time, the Hospitaller fortress surrounded, his fellow knights preparing to set fire to it. He hailed the senior Templar for the Kingdom of France. "Sir, I've discovered who's behind this, and it is *not* the Hospitallers."

Matthew's eyes widened. "Are you certain?"

"Absolutely." Marcus turned in his saddle and shouted toward the closed iron gates. "Hospitallers! Please send a delegation to talk! You must hear what I have to say before innocent blood is shed here today, and those who have conspired to destroy us both become victorious!"

Matthew repositioned as Marcus turned to face the gate. Nothing was said between them as Marcus' heart hammered from the hard ride here, and the desperation of the situation. If the Hospitallers refused to talk, there might still be war between the two greatest orders of

Christendom.

The gate creaked open and the leader of the Hospitaller contingent rode out with four guards. He came to a halt in front of Marcus, not even acknowledging Matthew, the animosity between the two obvious.

Marcus bowed in his saddle. "Sir, I am Sir Marcus de Rancourt. To whom do I have the honor of addressing?"

"I am Sir Bertrand de Montaigu. What is it you have to say, Sir Marcus? My patience is wearing thin."

"Thank you for your time, sir. And I must tell you, that what I am about to say I have not yet had a chance to convey to Sir Matthew, however given the situation, I feel it's necessary to share this information with both of you before it's too late."

Matthew waved his hand. "Proceed, Sir Marcus."

"Of course, sir. I'll start at the beginning. Back in Rome, where Sir Damase de Sissey was stationed, he discovered transactions that didn't balance, suggesting forged Letters of Credit."

"So, your code *was* broken!"

Marcus nodded at Bertrand. "Yes."

Matthew grabbed him by the arm. "Sir Marcus! Careful what you say."

"Sir, the only way to end this is to tell the entire truth. Trust me. When you hear what I have discovered, you will realize that nothing I reveal now is anything our Hospitaller friends won't know tomorrow."

Matthew bristled at the friends reference, but released Marcus' arm. "Very well, continue."

"Thank you. Sir Damase came here to investigate,

with the full authority of the Pope. He discovered a pattern where the forger would redeem the Letters of Credit in a ring around Paris, and later discovered that it was more than one person doing this. We discovered that a local gang, led by a man named Pequin, had discovered that a Mr. René Courvat had cracked our code, and what he was up to. Pequin took over the operation, substantially increasing the amounts being stolen over the past several months. Sir Damase managed to track down René, but was murdered."

"We had nothing to do with that!" interjected Bertrand, glaring at Matthew.

"No, you didn't."

Matthew cursed. "Are you sure?"

"Yes, sir. What I believe happened is that Sir Damase was indeed accosted by two Hospitallers. He killed one of them and the other escaped." Marcus turned to Bertrand. "Was the man killed one of yours?"

"Yes."

Marcus sighed. "Then that proves it."

Bertrand eyed him. "How?"

Marcus explained. "At this point, there was little chance you could have known about the breaking of the code."

Bertrand agreed. "We knew nothing until only moments ago."

"I believe you. For as I said, we've both been played."

"By who?" asked Matthew, now repositioned so he could address both Bertrand and Marcus, the horses of the three men all nose to nose.

"I'll get to that. I believe the attack on Sir Damase

was random, and had nothing to do with what is going on."

"Then who killed him?"

"I can't say for certain, though we did find another body near the scene. He was definitely not from any order of knights that I am aware of, for he was filthy and dressed in rags. No Templar, Hospitaller, or man from the order I believe is truly behind this would ever be caught in such a state."

Bertrand frowned. "So, it was just a brigand?"

Marcus shook his head. "No, I don't think so. We know Sir Damase had realized he had crossed paths with René only moments before, so gave pursuit. From what I've been told, René is not the sort that would kill. I believe he was being watched by Pequin's men, perhaps to make sure he didn't get caught. Whatever the case, when Sir Damase confronted him, I believe René's protectors intervened. One was killed, but another shot Damase in the back with a crossbow. We know René obviously returned to Paris early, as he was found in the Hospitaller hospital, therefore didn't complete his normal loop around the city. On our way back to Paris, we were attacked by six Hospitallers, who were specifically looking for me."

Simon, standing nearby, cleared his throat. "Whom we dispatched with ease."

Bertrand shook his head. "Impossible. I would have heard if six of our men were missing."

Marcus nodded. "I agree. The fact they were looking for me meant it wasn't a random attack. It was targeted. And only someone who knew where I was could know to take that road. They would either encounter me on it while I returned to Paris, or find me in the town I reported to the fortress as my last position."

Matthew leaned forward in his saddle. "So then how did they know?"

"We have a spy at the fortress."

Matthew sat up. "I knew it! Who?"

Marcus smiled slightly. "In a moment, sir."

Matthew growled. "You frustrate me, sir."

Bertrand chuckled. "I as well."

Marcus held up a hand. "It is important that you know everything, sirs. We returned to the fortress, were brought up to date by the sergeant on duty, and I noticed something odd about one of the stable boys who always seemed underfoot. I ordered him followed before we left to rendezvous with you at the hospital. When we arrived, you had already headed here, and our tracker found us. He led us to those truly behind everything."

"Who?" demanded Matthew.

"If you'll indulge me, I'll explain." Groans abounded. "Somehow, this other order found out about the code being broken. Now, the fact that the Hospitallers didn't know, suggests that it was only locals who knew. And we know one local who thought she could profit from this knowledge."

"Mrs. Thibault!"

Marcus glanced over his shoulder, surprised but pleased to see Thomas, flanked by his squires, the boy's mouth agape. "Exactly. Didn't you tell me she had discovered that René had broken the code, and that Pequin had found out and was using him?"

"Yes."

"And you said she had figured out some way to

profit from the knowledge, but refused to say what that was?"

"Yes. And after that, she sent me away. She told me to go to Crécy-la-Chapelle because it was too dangerous for me to stay."

"Would she normally be that scared of Pequin?"

Thomas shook his head. "I don't think so, though if she crossed him, perhaps."

"Exactly. I suggest something else is going on here. I suggest she realized she had a piece of information that was worth something. In fact, it was worth more than any of her normal contacts could afford. That meant she had to go to someone with deep pockets. Perhaps even someone she was indebted to."

"Who?" asked Bertrand and Matthew in unison.

"She went to those behind this, told them about René and how he had broken the code, was forging Letters of Credit, and how Pequin had found out and was now using him to do the same. The people she went to set a plan in motion to profit from it, but first, they had to confirm her story. They tried to kidnap René, but as we know, René was making his loop around the city. So instead, they went to Pequin's establishment and massacred them, no doubt interrogating them as they tried to find out where René was. Instead, they found his sisters, kidnapped earlier by Pequin's men. They took the sisters to use as leverage."

Matthew nodded. "Yes, I was told that he was asking about them when he awoke at the hospital. He accused Hospitallers of having taken them and of having beaten him nearly to death."

"Good. That means René was firmly convinced that

Hospitallers were behind everything, and there could be little chance of him being mistaken of so many things, which means that whoever was behind this was determined to make sure your order, Sir Bertrand, was the guilty party."

"But why us?"

"*That* is where this gets interesting."

Matthew grunted. "Really? *That* is where? Sir Marcus, the tale you have spun is remarkable, yet we are still no closer to knowing who is behind this."

Marcus bowed slightly. "You will in a moment, sir. Something critical was revealed by Pequin as he lay dying in front of us. Something I didn't think much of at the time, beyond the fact he had identified Hospitallers as the guilty parties. I should have realized it at the time, instead dismissing the critical detail of that conversation as merely the confusion of a dying man."

Bertrand edged closer. "What? What did he say?"

"He sent us to the home of Alain, one of his men, whom he felt might know where to find another one of his men who was following René. He described the house as being painted like the Hospitaller shield. A white cross on black. But when we went to the house, it was painted white, with a black cross on the door."

Matthew's jaw dropped and he exchanged a shocked look with Bertrand. "Teutons!"

Marcus smiled. "Exactly. Their colors are the opposite of yours, Sir Bertrand. I believe Pequin confused the two."

David rode forward. "That's right! When we were at the tavern earlier today, a survivor said that Pequin had said something like, 'I thought you Hospitallers were supposed to be men of honor,' and the man responded in an accent, so the witness wasn't sure what he said."

Bertrand grunted. "Probably a German accent."

Jeremy rushed forward. "That would explain their focus on you, sir! They wanted to kill you because of the fact you took down the German ambassador a few months ago in the adultery scandal."

Marcus' head slowly bobbed. "Perhaps. So, now we have a witness that claims Pequin, in his final moments, named his murderers, in their presence, as Hospitallers. And Pequin told me they were Hospitallers, despite the fact his description of their colors turned out to be Teutonic."

Bertrand gasped. "Those bastards! So, what you're saying is they attacked the bar wearing their Teuton colors, he calls them Hospitallers by mistake, they then get the idea that they can frame us, and proceed to move forward disguising themselves as Hospitallers!"

Marcus nodded. "Exactly. They let the mistaken rumor spread that Hospitallers were responsible for the attack on Pequin, and then sent men dressed in your colors to kill me." Marcus leaned closer. "Tell me, if you were to order an assassination like that, would you ever wear your colors?"

"As Hospitallers, we would never commit such an attack. It would be dishonorable." Bertrand held up his hand, cutting off Marcus' follow up question. "So, by extension, if anyone were to commit such an attack, one would never wear one's colors."

Marcus acknowledged the man's honesty. "Exactly. They wanted witnesses. They just didn't realize *we* would be the witnesses. They wanted word to get back to the fortress that Hospitallers had killed us, thus adding to our suspicions that you were behind everything. They obviously captured René while wearing your colors, beat him, then dropped him off at your hospital. They then sent the anonymous message to us telling us where to find him, and lo and behold, we find him in a Hospitaller location."

Matthew cursed. "Those Teuton bastards! They almost had us at war with each other."

Bertrand agreed. "What should we do?"

Matthew squared his shoulders. "There is only one thing we can do."

Bertrand turned his horse to face Matthew. "Agreed, but we must do it together."

Matthew smiled and extended his hand. "Agreed!"

Sir Gotfried's/Teutonic Order Headquarters
Paris, Kingdom of France

Sir Gotfried rose at the sound of a commotion below, heavy footfalls rushing up the stairs then down the hall that led to his office. His door burst open and Konrad charged in.

"Sir, they're here!"

Again without specifics!

"Who?"

"The Templars *and* the Hospitallers!"

Gotfried tensed as his body crawled with fear. "What? Together?"

"Yes, sir!"

"How is that even possible?"

"I don't know."

"How many?"

Konrad's eyes bulged. "All of them!"

Gotfried cursed. "How could you possibly know that?"

Konrad shrugged. "Well, it might as well be all of them. There are hundreds. We're surrounded. Someone must have talked. We had them at each other's throats. Someone must have told them the truth."

Gotfried slammed his fist on his desk. "Besides our men, all of whom I trust implicitly, only one person knew."

"Who?"

"Mrs. Thibault. She knew what was going on. She knew we were involved."

Konrad's eyes were wide. "She wouldn't dare!"

"Yet she must have, for no one else knew." He jabbed a finger at his second. "Take the tunnel. Kill her."

"But, sir, what about you?"

Gotfried reached for his sword. "I die with my brothers. If we are captured, they may make us talk, and the truth could damage the Order. But if we fight and die, then our honor, and our innocence, is maintained."

"But surely they'll say why they did it. You'll be dying uselessly."

Gotfried shook his head. "Will they? The Templars can never admit their code was broken, and I guarantee you, they either already have, or definitely will before this night is over, tell the Hospitallers that if they ever reveal the secret, they'll eliminate every last one of them in revenge. No, my friend, the secret of the Templar code being broken will die here tonight, preserving the honor of all three orders."

Konrad snapped to attention. "Sir Gotfried, you are the most honorable man I know. It has been a privilege."

Gotfried's chest tightened as he returned the honor. "As it has been mine. Now, eliminate Mrs. Thibault before she can tell anyone else of our involvement, and I will kill the sisters and burn their bodies. There can be no proof we were ever involved."

"Surrender now and I promise you a fair trial!" called Sir Matthew, the response shouted in German, something no doubt unsavory, followed by a volley of arrows erupting from the windows. Several Templars and Hospitallers alike went down, and Marcus turned to Matthew.

"We must attack now, before they have a chance to harm the sisters!"

Matthew agreed, raising his sword high in the air, then dropping it. "Forward!"

The men surrounding the building charged ahead, every ground level door and window assaulted at once, Marcus and Simon leading the way. Simon kicked down the main door with one swift motion and Marcus rushed past followed by David and Jeremy. Arrows were loosed by the expert archers as Marcus and Simon, along with a dozen other knights, faced stiff resistance in the foyer of the building.

Marcus and Simon, side-by-side, engaged two Teutons as the others paired off, more Templars and Hospitallers continuing to pour into the confined area. Marcus swung his sword, his attack expertly parried, then his opponent raised his sword high over his head, exposing his midriff, and Marcus stepped forward, thrusting his sword deep into the man's belly, twisting the blade before yanking it free.

He dropped to the floor and Marcus advanced, lifting his sword to his right and catching Simon's opponent off guard, leaving him exposed for his sergeant to finish him off. They advanced together, and Marcus noticed something odd.

They were winning.

Too easily.

These men are sacrificing themselves.

And while he had no problem with Teutons dying, they needed information. He rushed one of the few remaining, smacking his sword aside and instead of finishing him off, grabbed his hand bearing his sword and pinned it to the wall as Simon pressed his dagger blade against the man's neck.

"Where are the girls?" demanded Marcus.

The man glared at him. "What girls?"

Simon drew his blade across the man's throat, blood trickling as the man's eyes bulged. "Answer the man's question."

"In the basement!" He pointed to a door in the far corner. "Over there!"

Marcus withdrew and nodded at Simon who finished the job, the body collapsing to the ground in a heap as they cut across the room, the sword battles still in full swing as Teutons from the second floor joined their dying brothers.

Simon raised his foot to kick the door when Marcus reached forward and opened it. He grinned at his sergeant. "Sorry for depriving you of the satisfaction of destroying yet another thing that was in your way."

Simon reached up and tore the door from its hinges, tossing it aside. Then grinned. "Sorry, you were saying?"

Marcus laughed then rushed down the stairs that had been revealed, finding a series of doors that appeared to be prison cells, and at the far end a torch bouncing as if someone were running. He pointed. "It must be some sort of tunnel." The flame disappeared, signaling the successful escape of someone.

"Should I go after him?"

Marcus shook his head, knocking down the first door. "No, our priority is the sisters." There was a break in the noise from above and he took the opportunity. "Is there anybody down here?"

Gotfried held his prize dagger to Grace's throat, his hand held over her mouth, the older sister trembling in silence as the Templars or Hospitallers, it didn't matter which, searched outside the door. He was going to be caught, unless there was some diversion that drew their attention away.

He flinched as someone pounded on the door.

"Anyone in there?"

Vivienne whimpered.

He pressed the blade against her stomach and glared at her in the torchlight. She squeezed her eyes shut, shaking, but silent.

Suddenly the door flew open.

Marcus surged inside, sword drawn, the whimper of a little girl distinct despite the battle overhead. Simon rushed in after him, both splitting off to flank the Teuton bastard holding the girls hostage, a dagger to the neck of the youngest.

"Come any closer, and she dies!"

Marcus slowly circled. "Kill her, and I promise you I'll eviscerate you so slowly, you'll take days to die, with every one of your remaining moments spent in more pain than you can possibly imagine."

"Not very holy, for a monk," sneered the man.

"God shows no mercy for those who would harm children." Marcus continued advancing to the man's left, Simon to his right, forcing their prey to divide his attentions.

"I intend to die here tonight, Templar. And these girls must die."

"Why? Because they're proof of your order's

treachery?"

"I have no idea what you're talking about."

"Don't deny it. You've been behind everything. You were the ones who killed Pequin and his men, and once you realized that he thought you were Hospitallers, you pitted our two orders against each other, in the hopes we would destroy ourselves."

The man spat. "I admit nothing! And when this night is through, there will be none left alive to accuse."

Marcus smiled slightly. "So, you admit this was a rogue operation? That your masters in Venice had no idea what you were up to?"

"I admit to nothing!" He waved the dagger in front of him. "Kill me, Templar!"

Marcus shook his head. "No. Let the girls go, and answer for your crimes."

The Teuton pressed the knife against the little girl's neck. "If you don't kill me, then I'll kill them!"

"Committing suicide through us is still suicide, Teuton. You'll spend eternity burning in Hell."

The man laughed. "I'm going there anyway." He raised the dagger, stabbing the air between them, and Marcus acted. He surged forward, sword extended, and the man turned to fully engage his opponent when suddenly his eyes bulged and he cried out, his chest bursting forward before he sank to his knees, releasing the two girls from his grasp. They rushed for the door screaming as he collapsed, Simon's dagger, thrown perfectly, wedged between his shoulder blades, blood seeping out steadily as the Teuton's still beating heart assured his eventual death.

Marcus stood over him and kicked his weapon aside. "I guess you got your wish."

The man stared up at him. "My order will win in the end, Templar."

Simon spat. "But not today."

Thibault Residence
Paris, Kingdom of France

Simone sat in her chair, her eyes closed, a smile on her face as she thought of her wedding day, and how now, all that remained of that life were the happy memories.

Our debts are cleared, my love.

Her chest heaved as an image of his final moments threatened to tear her happiness asunder, but she managed to push it aside, instead returning to the moment in her life where she had been happiest, her entire future ahead of her with the man she loved.

Who knew then how horribly things would turn out?

The door downstairs creaked and she bolted upright in her chair as the sound of footfalls on the stairs echoed through the still house.

"Enzo? Is that you?"

There was no answer.

"Thomas?"

Again, no answer, yet the footfalls continued.

She rose, her heart fluttering as she put on her bravest voice. "Who's there? Answer me!"

And out of the shadows of the hallway emerged a Teuton Knight, in full regalia, his sword drawn.

"Sir Konrad!"

And she knew she was about to die.

But not without a fight.

She grabbed objects from her desk, pens, papers, paperweights, inkwells, anything she could throw, and hurled them at the advancing knight, all the while cursing him at the top of her lungs.

Yet it was all of no use as she found herself in a corner, the knight's sword pressed against her chest.

"Prepare to die."

She held up her hands, squeezing as deeply as she could into the corner, when she smiled. "No, *you* prepare to die."

Konrad's eyes narrowed. "What?"

"Look behind you."

He tilted his head to the side and frowned. "You don't expect me to fall for that, do you?"

She shrugged. "Fine. Don't look behind you."

Curiosity won out and he looked.

Enzo grabbed him by the head, lifting him from the floor and throwing him through the opposite wall. He turned to his mistress. "Are you unhurt, ma'am?"

She nodded, then flicked a finger toward the new hole in the wall. "Go have your fun."

He grinned. "Yes, ma'am."

The beating was brutal and extended, with several screams that sent chills down her spine as she straightened herself before returning to her chair. A few moments later, Enzo returned, something gripped in his hand.

"What's that?" She gasped. "Is that his arm?"

Enzo shrugged. "It came off, so I beat him with it." He grinned. "I've always wanted to do that."

Simone laughed, her head slowly shaking. "Thank God you're on my side, Enzo."

He bowed slightly. "Always."

She waved a hand at the disaster that was now her offices. "Next time, though, can you kill him without so much damage? This is going to cost me a fortune to fix."

Enzo frowned. "Is it coming out of my pay again?"

She chuckled. "Not this time, my friend, not this time."

Sir Gotfried's / Teutonic Order Headquarters
Paris, Kingdom of France

"They fought to the last man, sir. No survivors."

Matthew shook his head at Marcus' summary, surveying the sight as Templars and Hospitallers worked side-by-side, pulling the bodies from the building and tending to each other's wounded. He turned to Bertrand. "Your men fought well tonight, Sir Bertrand."

"As did yours, Sir Matthew. Let us hope that tonight marks a new beginning between our two orders."

Matthew bowed his head. "Let us hope, though I fear it shall not." He extended a hand. "But let it be a new beginning between the two of us."

Bertrand smiled, taking the hand. "If that is all to come of this night, then it will have still been a good one."

Marcus gestured toward the two sisters huddled nearby, two Hospitallers attending to them. "Sir, I think we should reunite them with their brother as quickly as possible."

Bertrand nodded. "I'll see to it personally."

"Thank you."

Matthew turned to Bertrand. "Needless to say, no one can ever know what truly happened here."

"You mean with respect to your code being broken?"

"Our code was never broken."

Bertrand laughed. "Of course it wasn't."

Matthew smiled. "Good. I think I'm going to enjoy our new relationship."

Bertrand slapped him on the back. "As am I! Now, if you'll excuse me, I have two young ladies to reunite with their brother." Bows were exchanged and Bertrand left to attend to the sisters.

Marcus sighed. "We got lucky today. This could very easily have gone a different way."

Matthew regarded him. "Oh, I think God sent us a guardian angel."

Marcus' eyebrows rose. "Who?"

"You, you fool! If you hadn't figured out what was going on, we would have attacked the Hospitaller fortification and we'd be finished, exactly as the Teutons wanted."

"I'm not so sure that's what was going on here."

"What do you mean?"

"I believe Sir Gotfried was acting alone, without the knowledge of the Teutonic leadership."

"Can you be sure?"

"No, though the fact everyone here, including Sir Gotfried, was so willing to die, suggests no one wanted to be interrogated."

Matthew nodded. "So no one could find out what they did."

"Exactly. If people outside this outpost knew, then there would be no point. Someone would eventually reveal their secret, and we would go to war with the Teutons, Templars and Hospitallers alike. But with everyone dead, there is nothing beyond hearsay to suggest they were involved."

"Then it's over."

"Let's hope." Marcus waved as Bertrand left with the sisters, both with their heads poked out the windows, blowing kisses at their saviors. "What now, sir?"

Matthew sighed. "Now, we bury our dead, and try to convince people that the rumors of our code being broken are just that."

Marcus smiled slightly. "I've got an idea about that."

De Rancourt Residence
Crécy-la-Chapelle, Kingdom of France

"So, how long will you be with us?"

Thomas shrugged at Lady Joanne's question. "I'm not sure. Mrs. Thibault wants me to stay here until things settle down. I guess there's a bit of a power struggle going on between those trying to fill the void created by Pequin's death. Normally there's always someone to take the place of someone like that within the organization, but the Teutons killed them all. The only one who survived was Alain, and there's no way he could take over."

"Why's that?" asked Beatrice as she poured everyone a tisane.

"He's, umm, not known as very bright. Mrs. Thibault has agreed to give him a job once his wounds heal."

"What happened to him?" asked Isabelle, sitting to his right, his hand clasped in hers.

"The Teutons beat him badly, along with René. The Hospitallers are taking care of them both."

"I really wish you'd just stay here and forget about that nasty woman."

Thomas flushed as his chest tightened. "Well, I may be here for a bit longer than I originally planned. Things aren't very safe right now."

Marcus smiled. "Good. Then you can help us work the farm and see what you think of it."

Thomas stared at his hands. "Umm, I suppose."

Jeremy held up his spoon. "And I'll teach you about using a shovel."

Thomas was afraid to respond. "I think I can figure that out."

"Oh, it's not *how* you use it that's interesting, it's *what* you use it to shovel."

Now he was certain he was afraid. "Such as?"

"Shit, my boy! Shit! That's half of farming. We feed the animals. They shit. We clean up their shit, then feed them again." Jeremy leaned forward and slapped him on the back. "And the job is all yours!"

"Gee, thanks."

Jeremy shook him by the shoulder. "Welcome to the bottom rung, my boy! The view is shit!"

Courvat Residence
Paris, Kingdom of France

"Mrs. Fromont is here to see you."

René sighed, steeling for what was ahead. He nodded at Vivienne. "Show her in."

Fromont entered, her hat in her hand, her eyes staring at the floor. "Good morning, René."

"Good morning, Mrs. Fromont. How can I help you?"

"I truly do hate to ask, and you know I wouldn't unless we were desperate, but is there any way you could see yourself forging another one of those Letters of Credit? This is the last time, I swear!"

"I'm afraid I can't."

Her eyes met his. "Why? Are you scared the Templars might find out?"

René shook his head. "No, that's not it. I really can't."

"Why?"

"Well, I *can't*. I never broke the code."

She eyed him. "What are you talking about? You gave me some Letters of Credit before and they worked."

He smiled. "I know, but those weren't forgeries."

Her eyes widened. "They were real? What do you mean?"

"I found them. A bunch of them. They were on a dead Templar messenger. I found him in the forest outside of the city. He had been thrown from his horse and snapped his neck. I took the Letters of Credit. They were already redeemed so had a manifest with the redeemers' names listed. All I did was figure out which name belonged to which Letter of Credit, and that was it. I just copied out the originals without the markings indicating they had already been redeemed. When it worked, I just kept doing it, a little at a time, and then when a few of you asked, I gave you some."

She shook her head, her mouth agape. "But why did you claim to have broken the code?"

His head sagged. "I was too ashamed to admit I had left a dead man without a proper burial, and had stolen from him as well."

Fromont backed away, shaking her head. "This is terrible. People are going to hear about this! There'll be no living it down, this!"

René frowned. "I know, I'm so ashamed."

Fromont left without saying another word, and when the door downstairs slammed shut, he smiled at his sisters as they rushed into the room.

"Do you think that did it?" asked Vivienne.

René stood. "She's such a gossip, I wouldn't be surprised if half the neighborhood already knows."

Giggles erupted from both girls.

"Now, is everyone packed?"

They both nodded firmly.

"Good." He patted the bag with his ill-gotten gains, gains the Templars had graciously allowed him to keep in exchange for playing his one final part. "Let's leave this wretched place, once and for all."

THE END

ACKNOWLEDGMENTS

While I was working on this novel, the Notre Dame Cathedral in Paris burned. I remember watching the live footage, shaking my head at the horrific scene.

History was burning.

And it made me think about just how at risk our irreplaceable artifacts are. The extent of the damage to the structure and its contents is still being determined, though initial reports are that it wasn't as bad as it could have been. But what about the National Museum in Brazil? It was a near total loss. And then, of course, there are the priceless artifacts and structures destroyed by Islamic fundamentalists like ISIS and the Taliban.

Our history is entrusted to governments and societies around the world, yet little thought is given to how well protected they are. What is mankind's responsibility when it comes to our past? Brazil and Notre Dame should be wakeup calls to better protect our history. We live in an age where we can digitally preserve, and physically reproduce, almost anything. Our history should be scanned and stored, so that in the future, should disaster strike, it can be at a minimum reproduced so accurately, people can still enjoy it.

For nothing lasts forever, if left to the whims of nature and man.

In 700 years, someone will want to write about our little portion of time, and I hope when their dad is doing the research, he has more to go on than the little tidbits mine did when it comes to things like Templar codes and ancient banking systems.

And speaking of, as usual, there are people to thank, or in this case, *a* person. My dad, as always, for the research, and no one else! That's right, this one, for some reason, didn't need any other outside help to write, beyond, of course, my wife, daughter, mother, and friends, for their continued support, and the proofreading and launch teams!

To those who have not already done so, please visit my website at www.jrobertkennedy.com, then sign up for the Insider's Club to be notified of new book releases. Your email address will never be shared or sold.

Thank you once again for reading.